Another Death in Venice

Sarah's heart bleeds for the troubles of the world – its violence, torture, poverty, famine.

Michael on the other hand prefers life as seen through the view-finders of his favourite film-directors. He dislikes suffering humanity in general and the other people on his Italian package holiday in particular. But circumstance and Sarah get him involved despite himself – with a battered wife, an Italian boy, a jealous husband, two Florentine whores, and a strange pair of drifters who join the group at Sarah's instigation.

In Venice things get worse with a near-drowning, a botched seduction, an accusation of poisoning, a beating-up, and Michael being questioned by the police about a murder and the films of Fred Astaire. More serious still are the questions Sarah is asking about their marriage. And by the end of the book she at least knows what real blood looks like.

R

by the same author

FELL OF DARK
A CLUBBABLE WOMAN
AN ADVANCEMENT OF LEARNING
A FAIRLY DANGEROUS THING
RULING PASSION
A VERY GOOD HATER
AN APRIL SHROUD

Another Death in Venice

Reginald Hill

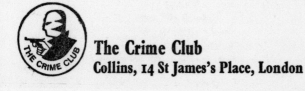

The Crime Club
Collins, 14 St James's Place, London

William Collins Sons & Co Ltd
London · Glasgow · Sydney · Auckland
Toronto · Johannesburg

First published 1976
© Reginald Hill 1976
ISBN 0 00 231015 5
Set in Monotype Baskerville
Made and Printed in Great Britain by
William Collins Sons & Co Ltd Glasgow

PART I

RIMINI

I

During the night, the plump woman in the gipsy wig cried again in the next bedroom. Sarah lay and listened, full of concern, but did not waken Michael who had declared two days earlier that of all forms of reveille to this sad and sorry world, he found a fat woman's weeping the most deplorable.

After a while the noise stopped or moderated sufficiently to be subsumed by the unceasing hum of traffic. Someone somewhere was having the late night fun promised by the brochures, or perhaps just driving around in search of it.

Michael had been smoking in bed earlier and the stench still hung on the air. Sarah thought of tiptoeing on to the balcony and staring forty-five degrees left at the view of the Adriatic which was costing them 300 lire per day extra. (This payment troubled her disproportionately, making her think of the disaster-struck in so many parts of the world trekking to the ocean's edge and peering out hopelessly over the empty waters.) But before she could rise, the picture dissolved into rhythmic waves and she fell asleep.

At breakfast, Michael watched burly Bob Lovelace eat his English fry-up (600 lire extra).

'I had a dream last night,' he said.

'Are you going on the beach today?' Sarah asked Molly Lovelace, an attractive, rather nervous girl who seemed so intimidated by Michael that she had hardly spoken during the three days they had shared the table. Her husband was different. He did not speak at all, but from choice rather than nerves.

'I dreamt that I was sitting at breakfast just like now,

and everyone in the room was chatting away about the beach, and booking a spot, and what was for lunch, when suddenly a huge voice boomed out, as if from a megaphone, crying, "Oh no, no, no, no! Cut! Cut! Cut!" We all looked up and out there, beyond the swimming pool, somewhere out over the sea, we became aware of a huge figure, just an outline, like someone seen in the aureole of an arc-light. "Oh no!" this figure cried. "That was terrible. That will never do. Let's try it again." "From the beginning?" we all asked hopefully. "No," came the answer. "Just from where you come down for breakfast. But this time, with *feeling*."

'Then I woke up.'

Bob rolled a rasher of bacon into a fatty cylinder and thrust it into his mouth. Molly stared at Michael in alarm.

'Take no notice,' said Sarah brightly. 'My husband's always making up dreams.'

'Aren't we all?' asked Michael.

Their attention was diverted by the arrival of the plump woman in the gipsy wig whose entrances, always some minutes before her husband's, had assumed an almost ceremonial significance for the other guests. The previous evening she had been like an overweight Garbo crossing the foyer of Grand Hotel with many a *distrait* backward glance. This morning dressed in a close-fitting black beach robe relieved by a multi-stranded coral necklace, her eyes deep shadowed in a Quant-pale face, she progressed down the room like the prow of a stately funeral ship, looking neither to left nor right. Bette Davies as Elizabeth the First, thought Michael.

Her husband who appeared five minutes later was a spare, gangling man with a self-satisfied smile who paused half a dozen times to exchange reminiscences of his last night's excesses.

Molly was among his chosen confidantes.

'Good morning, my dear,' he cried resting his hand familiarly on her bare shoulder. 'And how are you? You look well enough, I must say, but you don't deserve to, not the way you were putting it away. Only joking! But Bob here's the man. What a gullet! What was it, Bob?

Fifteen pints of Italian beer and he's still having his eggs and bacon! I'll try a coffee, I think. See you later. With a bit of luck we might get a bit of sunshine today.'

With a friendly nod at Sarah and Michael he joined his wife, who greeted his arrival by moving her chair two feet back from the table and lighting another cigarette.

'Let's be off, darling,' said Michael. 'Or we'll miss the best of the day.

'That's the bit,' he explained to Molly, 'before the sun gets too hot and while there's no more than one square Englishman to every square yard.'

'You shouldn't victimize that girl,' said Sarah as they left the dining-room.

'You shouldn't patronize her,' said Michael.

'I don't,' she protested. 'Someone's got to talk to her and that brute she's married to never opens his mouth except to stick food into it.'

'That,' said Michael, 'is because he is a typical representative of the British lower orders.'

Torn between her militant feminism and her militant socialism, Sarah fell silent. Michael accepted as triumph what was merely truce and watched her with an indulgent smile as she methodically ticked off her list of beach essentials. Bathing cap, Biros, books; Lilo, Lilo pump; nose-protector; pocket repair outfit, postcards; sun glasses, sun lotion . . .

Michael grew impatient. His smile was as deep as his indulgence went. He stepped into the bathroom and began to clean his teeth in mineral water.

'Must we go on the beach today?' he asked through pink foam. 'Couldn't we give it a miss?'

'Next week we'll roam around Venice till we're pools of butter in St Mark's Square,' Sarah answered. 'This part of the holiday's for swimming, tanning and relaxing.'

In fact she was as bored as he was but one triumph in a morning was more than enough for him. She suspected he really enjoyed lying on the beach more than she did but there was no easy way of moving out of the roles they had chosen when their Italian holiday was first discussed.

'At least couldn't we stay by the pool today?' he coaxed.

'And avoid all that sand.'

'England's full of swimming pools,' she said firmly. 'But the sea there rarely reaches seventy degrees Fahrenheit.'

He followed her through the door trailing the half-inflated Lilo behind him.

'That tan will get you blackballed when they see it at the Trades and Labour Club,' he said.

She wasn't listening. Their plump neighbour was on the point of entering her room, and with a sinking heart Michael realized his wife was about to engage her in conversation.

His first instinct was to go on alone, but he stifled it and instead came to a halt a few feet beyond the two women and looked out of a window, whistling the latest pop tune which several hundred juke-box playings had printed indelibly on his mind. His imminence would have no effect at all on Sarah, but there was always the chance that the other woman might react to his presence by going away. In any case, it was worth hearing what Sarah said. A timely interruption might prevent some complete disaster, such as an invitation for this outlandish creature to spend the day with them.

'Hello,' said Sarah brightly. 'We're in the room next door.'

'Are you?' replied the woman.

'Yes. I was just admiring your necklace. It's gorgeous. It's coral, isn't it?'

'That's right. Some tat I picked up in Benidorm last year. You can have it if you like it. I'm tired of the bloody thing. It keeps snagging my blouses.'

She began unfastening the necklace and Sarah looked with alarm at Michael, who grinned at her.

'No, really, I couldn't,' said Sarah. 'Honestly. It must have been quite expensive.'

'I'm not trying to sell you it,' snapped the woman, ceasing her efforts. Michael felt himself warming to her. The function of natives had always been to eat missionaries.

The woman spoke with a mild Midlands accent. She must, thought Michael, be in her forties, perhaps five or six years older than Sarah and himself. The deep mask of make-up and the jet black wig with its three ringlets pendant over either ear made a more accurate dating difficult.

'Is he yours?' asked the woman, looking at Michael.

'Yes, I suppose he is,' said Sarah. Michael stepped forward instinctively. A quick introduction and off seemed possible.

The woman nodded at him and turned back to Sarah.

'I don't like men,' she said. 'Does he have affairs? I think they all do, don't you?'

'Well, perhaps not all,' said Sarah. 'They like to pretend a bit. I'm Sarah Masson, by the way. And this is Michael.'

'I'm Wendy Trueman.'

'Oh. And your husband?'

'What about my husband?'

'What do they call him?'

'You find a name bad enough and I'll call him that,' said Wendy emphatically. 'Swine, they're all swine.'

To Michael's alarm her eyes began to fill with tears. He seized Sarah's arm.

'We'd better get our spot,' he said jovially. 'The Krauts will have been out there for hours and once the Wops and their bambinos arrive, we'll end up by the beach bar again.'

As anticipated, his racial smears distracted Sarah's attention from the tearful woman long enough for him to pull her a couple of steps down the corridor.

'See you later, Wendy,' he called to emphasize their departure.

The plump woman gave him a look of what might have been hatred or despair and went into her room.

Michael released Sarah and prepared to receive a tirade of recrimination. Instead she walked quietly by his side for a few moments.

'Poor woman,' she said finally, then added, '*Do* you have affairs?'

'Not *affairs*,' he said. 'Just the one. It's well known that for years I've been screwing the arse off that little black typist in the registry.'

He raised his voice as he spoke and she shushed him angrily and became silent herself. He smiled complacently at his own ability to reduce Sarah to something like the quiet, shy girl he had fallen for fifteen years earlier, though the quality of uncritical admiration was not repeatable. He was in fact uncertain precisely how his wife did regard him now. He had been content to accept that she thought of him as a traitor in the great class struggle, or, at best, shell-shocked. But a couple of months earlier he had come across some notes she had made for an extra-mural course in psychotherapy she was following and had been disturbed to find she was using him as a case-history. Anonymously and fictitiously, of course, and embellished by one or two hyperbolical features such as suspected schizophrenia and latent homosexuality, but nevertheless recognizably based on things he had done and said. He did not feel betrayed or anything as absurd as that, merely perturbed that she could have reached this objective standpoint without his noticing. They still loved each other, he believed, but he was no longer sure what precisely love meant.

To reach the beach they had to cross a road. Much has been written of Italian drivers but even the most vitriolic pen could not do them injustice. Michael refused to let the more timid Sarah hold his hand on the grounds that at crisis moments they inevitably disagreed on policy and she would get them both killed. So as usual he ended up on the beach side of the road while she was still waiting for a gap. He sat on a low wall and watched the morning procession to the sea. It was like the Sunday progress to church in the small Lancashire town where he had been born; the family groups, the uniformity of dress, the singleness of purpose, the certainty of reception; even the same faint shadows of anticipated boredom.

A hand grasped his shoulder. Turning, he looked at a broad, brown and extremely muscular belly. Dark hairs strayed up from the tartan trunks and spread like couch-grass round the navel. Raising his eyes he found himself looking up at Bob.

'Hello, Bob,' he said, thinking that Michaelangelo

would have admired the set of those shoulders and the
way the muscle flexed like steak beneath the sun-tanned
skin of the upper arm.

'You,' said Bob. 'Watch it. All right?'

'Well, all right,' said Michael.

It was only when Bob's hand let go of his shoulder that
he realized how tight the grip had been.

'What was Bob saying?' asked Sarah who had at last
crossed the road.

'I'm not sure. He told me to watch it.'

'You've been asking for it, the way you treat Molly,'
said Sarah.

'Anyway, I think I've solved the problem of Bob's job,'
answered Michael.

For some reason even Sarah's most subtle questioning
had not been able to elicit Bob's profession from Molly.
Michael had speculated that he was a heavily disguised
brain-surgeon, fearful of being bombarded with symptoms.

'He's not a brain surgeon at all,' continued Michael,
rubbing his shoulder. 'He's a film star. Queen Kong, the
gay gorilla.'

'For God's sake, Michael! And what on earth do you
think *you* are?'

Indignantly she marched towards the sea and, with an
aggressiveness uncharacteristic in her dealings with
foreigners, took possession of a beach umbrella right under
the noses of a family of Germans. They muttered angrily
and looked as if they might re-group for another attack
till Michael dropped the Lilo at their feet, smiled at them
and said with an expansive gesture, 'Lebensraum.'

He blew up the Lilo while Sarah, curiously prudish
still, wriggled out of her beach robe and looked defiantly
around as though her Marks and Spencer bikini would be
an immediate object of censure and lust. She had a
pleasant, rather boyish figure and as she anointed herself
with oil, Michael wondered what had happened to the
pneumatic girls of his adolescent dreams.

He untangled a deck chair and began to write a post-
card.

Dear Timmy and Toni, he began.

There once was a bishop of Rimini
Who profited so much from simony
That he bought shares in God
And to Jesus he said,
'*You can push off. From now on it's Him'n'me.*'

'Who are you writing to?' asked Sarah.

'Our children. You don't imagine I shall send postcards to anyone else?'

'Let me see.'

She reached out an oily hand and took the card.

'Why do you always have to be so clever? They won't understand a word.'

'Timmy's eleven and Toni is nearly ten. At their age I was getting pre-pubertal thrills from eighteenth-century novels.'

'Ha ha,' said Sarah. 'Your mother says you were a very slow child. And "said" doesn't rhyme with "God". Do you think they'll be all right?'

'I should think so. A parentless fortnight with the promise of exotic presents at the end of it – what greater joy this side Paradise?'

The decision to go on holiday without the children had not been taken lightly. Michael had worked at it for weeks, applying himself in true scholarly fashion to an examination of all Sarah's text-books on child care in order to muster evidence for his scheme. Spock's retractions had nearly caught him out, but Sarah had finally capitulated, convinced more by his fervour than his arguments. The children were still too young for her to be willing to precipitate a crisis. Michael had wanted Venice, Sarah had insisted on a beach but the Lido had been too expensive. Then Michael had discovered this two-centre holiday, five days each in Venice and Rimini, 'where Fellini was born and *I Vitelloni* is set,' he enthused. It fell just within their budget, and before she could find time in her busy life to consider what was happening, Sarah found herself at Luton Airport, full of concern at leaving the children with their reactionary grandma and fuller of hurt at their lack of concern.

But three days in the sun had salved both hurt and

concern, and now she returned the card to Michael and settled on the Lilo to toast her underdone parts. Michael glanced at his watch. His duty it was to warn her when to turn. He also regulated their overall beach timetable. It was rather like being at school. There was a period for swimming, one for drinking, one for going out in a paddle-boat, one for playing knock-out whist; plus a couple of free periods in which he could relax and consider abstract problems such as why it was so many lesser talents seemed to have got so many better jobs, which precise part of the beach Fellini had used in his film, and what it would be like to be seduced by Sophia Loren in a gondola. He had tried conjuring up a fantasy in which *he* did the seducing, but found it impossible. It didn't bother him, though he knew it would have bothered Sarah if he'd told her. But then she lacked his realism. In a world so manifestly unjust and simoniacal, it was a wise man who knew his place.

At dinner that night a shock awaited them. They had skipped lunch as usual, preferring a pair of luscious peaches to the three indifferent courses the hotel kitchen offered, so perhaps the switch had been performed then. Their table was empty when they arrived, but as they sat down Michael noticed Bob and Molly at the far side of the room.

'Isn't that where Gipsy Rose Lee sits?' he said to Sarah.

'Yes. Oh Michael, this is awful, you've frightened the poor girl off.'

This was unjust he felt, but even if he had been at fault he did not merit the punishment that followed.

'Hello,' said Wendy sitting heavily opposite him but addressing Sarah. 'God, but it's warm. You'd think they'd be able to serve hot soup, wouldn't you, but they never do.'

She lit a cigarette and drew deeply on it, furrowing her heavily spread magenta lipstick. She was wearing a long purple dress with a silk sunflower at the nadir of its deep cleavage. Michael dragged his eyes away from the land-slide of breast thus displayed; its light powdering of talc reminded him of the dusting of icing sugar with which his mother had consummated her Swiss rolls. Suddenly he tasted jam.

'What happened to Bob and Molly?' he asked.

'We like a bit of company,' said Wendy in an off-hand fashion. 'They don't seem to mind. She doesn't say much, does she?'

'She's very shy,' said Sarah defensively.

'Is she? She looks worn out to me. I don't expect he gives her much rest. He looks the type. But they're all the same, aren't they? One track.'

She looked at Michael as she spoke, not challengingly but with the resigned weariness of a nit-nurse in a slum-school.

'Hello, hello!'

It was the husband with his quiz compère smile.

'So we've been passed fit for human consumption! That's grand. Give us another year and the waiters might start speaking. It's Mike and Sarah, isn't it? I thought so. I always do a roll-call soon as I arrive any-where. Force of habit. I'm Wilf, Wilf Trueman. You've met the wife. Nice of you to let us join you. Hey, Mario! *Una bottiglia di vino.* This one's on me, I insist. *Grande bottiglia*, Mario. My usual.'

Michael caught Sarah's eye and was pleased to see his own horror reflected there. But he realized that the slightest sign of acerbity on his part would drive her into a compensatory excess of sweetness and light with God knew what unbearable results.

He held out his hand.

'Glad to meet you, Wilf.'

Wilf took the proffered hand, shook it, then gave it a squeeze and a twist.

'Just testing,' he said. 'I like to know if my new friends are masons or poofs. Well, Sarah, I don't think he wears an apron, but I'm not sure about a skirt. Just joking, old man.'

'For God's sake!' said Wendy, stubbing out her cigarette and lighting another.

'What's your line, Mike?' asked Wilf. 'How do you butter the bread?'

'I work in a Poly. A Polytechnic, that is. I'm a lecturer.'

'Well, well,' chuckled Wilf. 'I guessed something like that. Stands out a mile. Mind you, it's not really fair. Some might say, it takes a one to know a one.'

With a sinking heart Michael awaited the revelation that he was sharing a table with the Provost of King's.

'Are you a lecturer too?' asked Sarah.

Wendy coughed derisively.

'What? No! I lecher a bit, you might say, nudge, nudge. No, I have a little business. A few little businesses actually. Butchers. That's why I like to meat people, eh! But I know something about the teaching game. I'm on the council, deputy chairman of the Education Committee this year, so we're in the same line in a way, you and me, Mike.'

He grinned triumphantly before going on.

'What's your subject, Mike? No. Let me guess. Arithmetic. You look a calculating kind of chap. Right?'

'No,' said Michael. 'I'm in the department of communications media. I specialize in cinema.'

'Well, well. They pay you for that, do they? I like a good picture, mind you. Here, I saw this one the other week, *Midnight in the Dorm*, do you know it? Never mind, I'll tell you all about it some time when we're by ourselves.'

Michael smiled wanly at this threat, a smile which became a rictus of pain when he saw the huge plastic bottle of sweet white wine which Mario was depositing on the table.

He tried to refuse on the grounds of a delicate stomach, but Wilf insisted the more, asserting its therapeutic qualities like a shareholder.

'Which party do you represent?' said Sarah.

'Party? You can stick your parties, no offence. I belong to a ratepayers' group. I've got the small businessmen behind me. What have your parties ever done for them?'

The question was rhetorical, but Sarah, who spent half her life (Michael alleged) pushing socialist literature through letter-boxes, was more than willing to answer it. Michael, appreciating now why Wendy preferred to sit a couple of yards away, pushed back his own chair and smiled politely at her. She looked back at him with an expression so remote that he wondered if she were on some kind of drug.

'I think the price of things has gone up ridiculously,' she suddenly said.

'Ah. You've been here before?'

'Yes. Benidorm and Dubrovnik. Profiteering.'

'Ah,' said Michael again. He had a feeling that this was not a conversation to pursue, but the habit of precision was part of his job.

'The economies of Spain and Jugoslavia used to stand in a very low relationship to ours,' he explained. 'Though of course that is no longer the case.'

'Some bastard's making money. Whisky here is more expensive than at home. Do you know that?'

'Yes. I suppose it would be. But there are some very palatable Italian brandies at very reasonable prices.'

'I don't like brandy.'

The arrival of the first course drew them back to the table.

'Don't eat over-hearty,' advised Wilf. 'Leave some space for the chicken and chips.'

'I'm sorry?'

'The barbecue. You're going to the barbecue, aren't you?'

Sarah and Michael exchanged alarmed glances.

'Everyone goes to the barbecue!' said Wilf. 'You'll look very stand-offish if you don't come. Very stand-offish.'

How soon he had found the right buttons to press, thought Michael admiringly as a look of guilt replaced Sarah's alarm.

'We haven't got tickets,' she said. 'It must be booked up.'

'In any case,' began Michael, who frequently had occasion to deplore his wife's use of the refusal conditional when a little extra effort would produce the refusal absolute. But it was too late. Wilf was out of his seat and heading for the small side dining-room where the hotel courier and reception staff ate their, it was alleged, very superior meals. He returned triumphant with two pieces of cardboard which he tucked into the neck of Sarah's sun-top.

'There we are,' he said. 'Just call me Mr Fixit.'

'He can fix anything that doesn't matter,' said Wendy to no one in particular.

The barbecue coach came as they were drinking coffee. It had already picked up holidaymakers from other hotels and looked quite crowded, but in the event only five couples from the Leonardo climbed aboard.

'There must be a lot of stand-offish people here,' observed Michael drily to Sarah.

'Fortnighters,' said Wilf from the seat behind. 'They all went last week, I expect. That's how I heard it's so good.'

It was unspeakable. They sat at trestle tables in what looked like a derelict smallholding which had specialized in chickens and pigs. The chickens had probably died of undernourishment, or worse, and were shortly served enshrouded in their own grease. To wash this down, the clients were invited to help themselves freely from a huge barrel of wine which turned out to be like Wilf's usual – white, warm, weak and sweet.

There was dancing too, with music supplied by a group in peasant costume who, after a token gesture towards their own country with *Arrivederci Roma*, began to run through the whole gamut of English Palais music from the Military Two-step to the Conga. There were three elements present, Michael realized, the 'Come Dancing' lot who did their tailor's dummy pirouettes wearing fixed grimaces like royalty with piles; then the non-contact shake-and-wagglers; and finally the Italian youths who clearly came to every barbecue and stood overlooking the dancing like bored satyrs till they found a partner to clasp tightly and (he guessed) painfully as they swayed slowly in time to rhythms other than the band's.

Wilf had carried Sarah off into the maelstrom and Michael felt he had to ask Wendy. His intention was to shake-and-waggle but the press was so intense that it soon became a choice between complete separation or close contact. He took her in his arms with some reluctance but she was soft and warm and the experience soon became so voluptuous that the strains of a conga came as both relief and intrusion. He lost touch with Wendy in the subsequent reshuffling and found himself clinging to a behind which his gentle probings told him didn't begin to compare in terms of shape or texture.

Suddenly he was shouldered violently aside.

'I've warned you before,' growled Bob taking his place in the line. The woman ahead looked round and Michael now saw it was Molly.

'Sorry,' he said. It was, he realized, both too little and too much.

He looked around the dance floor but could not spot Wendy, nor for that matter Wilf and Sarah, so he returned to his seat via the bar where those who could not stomach the free wine paid exorbitant prices for more potable liquor.

The bitterness of his Campari-soda was a pleasant antidote to the wine, and for a few minutes with his eyes half-closed he was almost able to transform the setting into some sophisticated Roman night-spot where the *dolce vita* had been going on for two thousand years.

Then the band launched into 'Roll Out The Barrel' and he was back to reality. The others had still not returned and he made his way once more to the bar. This was situated behind the bandstand in a kind of concrete blockhouse which might have been purpose-built for security reasons or just left behind by the Germans in 1944. As he approached he saw Bob at the bar and, reluctant to risk again the man's inexplicable truculence, Michael moved behind the building to wait till he had left.

Suddenly he was back in Italy. The music, changed now to a gentle waltz, was merely a background to the richness of the night. Out there waiting was . . . who? Mangano, perhaps; Magnani; Monica Vitti; Giulietta Masina . . .

It is dark. Cicadas grate. A woman giggles. The camera grows used to the dark as the human eye does. Lines of vines emerge, wreathed around wires strung between posts. Among them here and there, white beneath the moon, human limbs wreath around each other also.

He moves forward, carefully but eagerly. Somewhere in another aisle a match splutters. Through the leaves a woman's face is visible for a moment, lips red and sensual, teeth bright in the moist open mouth.

'Why don't you all sod off?' said a weary voice.

Michael halted. He knew that voice.

A man said something in Italian, too rapidly for Michael's sub-title linguistics, and there was an outburst of laughter. There were about half a dozen of them. He guessed they were the young pseudo-Byrons who hung around the dance floor.

The man's voice came again.

'Signorina, come, I will show you a nice place, these others no good. Come.'

'Just sod off, I say. All of you.'

It was definitely Wendy. Michael was uncertain what to do. He hardly knew the woman, didn't want to get to know her better and if she cared to wander around in the dark with these youngsters, that was her business.

On the other hand she didn't sound as if she wanted their company.

'Signorina,' murmured the Italian urgently. 'Please, you come, eh, signorina?'

Signorina! Michael grinned. He was wasting his time with that subtle bit of flattery, he thought. He was both right and wrong.

'I'm not signorina, I'm signora,' declared Wendy. 'So go and find someone your own age, sonny.'

Enough of this must have got across to the others to cause a general laugh at the wooer's expense and he was provoked to seize Wendy's arm as she tried to brush him aside.

'Oh, get your greasy fingers off me,' she said. There was no panic in her voice, and while one part of Michael's mind told him his intervention was more likely to cause trouble than curb it, another part assured him this was the logic of cowardice and sent him moving forward.

'Evening, Wendy,' he said in his best Noel Coward casual voice. 'Everything all right?'

'Who's that? Oh, it's you,' said Wendy ungraciously.

'The bus will be going soon,' said Michael. 'The dance is over.'

It was true. The strains of the waltz had faded away and been replaced by the shuffling of feet and the hoarse roar of diesel engines.

Wendy stepped away from the young Italian and Michael sighed with relief. Then she screamed, twisted half round, lost her balance and fell into the young man's arms. Michael rushed forward and pulled her free.

'Go back to the car park,' he said steadily. She walked away and the young man tried to brush past Michael, who grasped him by the pocket of his wine-red sports shirt. It felt rather expensive. The youngster pulled away and he heard the pocket tear. Now the boy turned on him angrily and for a moment they stood face to face.

'OK, blue-eyes,' said Michael.

They locked arms round each other like a pair of Cumberland wrestlers and crashed to the ground, Michael on top. He felt the boy's sinewy body go limp beneath him and at the same time he had a sudden panicky awareness of the other youths all crowding around him. Pushing himself upright, he whirled round, ready to defend himself. They hadn't moved but remained in an interested row along one of the vines. Gathering his Anglo-Saxon dignity together, he strolled after Wendy. He had, he felt, done rather well.

'Are you all right?' he asked her again.

'I hate those bloody things,' she said.

'Well,' he said, as judiciously as became a victor, 'there's good and bad, I suppose. They're not very old.'

'What's that got to do with it? Once they're in your hair, who cares if they're ancient or have just been hatched?'

Her choice of metaphor puzzled then perturbed him.

'What are you talking about?' he asked.

'Those awful insects. Ciceros. What do you think?'

'Cicadas,' he said. 'Oh Jesus. Is that why you screamed?'

'It got right in my hair,' she said.

Michael looked round with a mixture of unease and

guilt. Only the rows of vines scratched the velvet darkness, but out there was a young *mafioso* with good grounds for a bitter vendetta. No, that was an absurd over-dramatization. More probably he was the son of some respected local citizen who was at this moment ringing the *carabinieri* to complain of this unprovoked assault by a drunken foreigner.

'I thought he'd grabbed you,' he said feebly, but she had moved on and it struck him that she probably hadn't even noticed the brief moment of violence.

In the barbecue area the holiday-makers were still moving in slow files to the bus park. Some, Michael noticed with a shudder, in a desperate effort to get their money's worth were standing by the wine-vat filling and refilling their goblets. He suddenly recalled a childhood trip to Blackpool to see the lights. The one image that remained to him was of an endless tunnel of flashing neon jammed solid with coaches, with human heads being sick through every window.

'Hello, hello! What's been going on here then?'

It was Wilf, very jovial, standing with his arm round Sarah's shoulders and his small bright-glinting eyes flickering from his wife to Michael.

Wendy ignored him.

'A breath of fresh air,' said Michael.

'Fresh air? In this country. *Fresh* air!'

'Michael's been very kind to me,' snapped Wendy.

Sarah tried to raise her eyebrows quizzically. Her thin over-mobile face lacked the control necessary for such subtleties and she merely looked startled.

'Anyone seen my missus?'

It was Bob, sweating profusely in his muscle-taut tee-shirt. For so possessive a man, thought Michael, he really was extremely careless with the girl.

'Molly? No,' said Wilf. 'Probably went for a stroll, old son. V. noisy it got in here. V. noisy *you* got! Where do you put it all, eh? No, she'll have gone for a breath of *fresh* air. Mike, you didn't spot her when you were out there enjoying your *fresh* air?'

Michael shook his head. Wilf's suggestive intonation had

not been lost on Bob but words were not going to help.

'Hadn't we better get back to the bus?' said Sarah. One of her pet phobias was being late and missing things. Michael usually would have made some crack but not tonight. The Leonardo was beginning to feel like some corner of a foreign beach which was as near to England, home, and safety as he could hope for tonight.

On the coach he found that Wilf had manipulated him into sitting next to Wendy while he and Sarah shared a seat a few places back. Was this wife-swapping, Education Committee style? The coach was delayed because Bob and Molly had not yet turned up.

'I hope they're all right,' said Michael, recalling his own experience. On reflection, if Bob found his wife being chatted up by any of the local lads, it was the locals he felt sorry for. He peered out of the window to see if he could spot them. The other half-dozen coaches had all started to move and were disputing the exit with much gunning of engines and hooting of horns. A figure was running from one coach to another, then slowly moving down the line of windows scrutinizing the faces inside. With a quite disproportionate shock of fear, Michael recognized him as the boy he had attacked. The red shirt was unmistakable. Whether his motive was immediate personal revenge or simple legal identification he couldn't guess. He took out his handkerchief and mopped his face, partly out of necessity, partly as concealment. But with Wendy sitting next to him, concealment was futile.

A cheer went up. Bob and Molly had arrived. She smiled shyly at their reception, he glowered, then both were thrown into their seat as the driver, who had been muttering impatiently to himself, released the clutch pedal and the coach bounded forward. As the vehicle squeezed through the narrow gate, the Italian boy appeared at the window. He recognized Wendy and, beyond her, Michael. His mouth opened in an inaudible shout and he rapped on the glass. Wendy looked down at him with total indifference. Michael tried to compose his features into an expression of conciliatory rue. The coach gathered speed. The youth ran alongside for a few yards, then was carried back into the darkness by the rushing road and Michael relaxed in his seat and tried to rationalize his fear. Behind him Wilf began to sing 'Show Me The Way To Go Home', and gradually other voices took up the burden, singing the words with a tipsy vigour which permitted no hint of irony.

That night it was Michael who awoke in the early hours to hear Wendy sobbing. It was not the noise that had disturbed him, but a slight nausea brought on, he diagnosed, by a combination of drink and fright. The crying stopped for a moment and he heard voices. Then it started again. He sat up in bed and Sarah turned over muttering, 'What's the matter?'

'It's Wendy. She's weeping again.'

'Uh-huh? Well, let her weep.'

She pulled the single sheet over her head and went back to sleep. Michael too subsided and lay awake, listening till he was certain his feeling of sickness was not going to necessitate getting out of bed. He put his arm round Sarah's naked body but the night was too warm for the contact not to become quickly uncomfortable, so he turned away, started counting men whose top jobs he could do standing on his head, and after fifty fell asleep.

II

Sarah was a physical prude though her intellectual scheme of things did not admit the notion of prudery. Frank and open discussions about sex had to be entered into with a smile, but she recognized that she heartily disliked them. Another person who recognized this was her dearest and oldest friend, Avril Hadley, who took great delight in countering Sarah's social conscience with her own super-sexuality. Empathetic tears for Asian orphans would still be staining Sarah's cheeks when Avril, with a cunning twist of the conversation, would bring to light her latest orgasmic ecstasy, substantiated whenever she and her husband spent the night at the Massons by the odd long, juddering, climactic cry, which Michael in one of his more endearing moments had suggested was learned from a set of Linguaphone records.

Avril was merely an irritant, but Sarah's present problem could turn into an embarrassment. It was all a matter of trying to react like the person she ought to be rather than the person she regrettably was. When Wilf had pressed himself against her on the dance floor and made sure she recognized his physical excitement, her first reaction had been to make an indignant exit. Then, reacting against the reaction, she had merely endeavoured to put a bit of distance between them, a manoeuvre he acknowledged with a complacent smile. On the coach on the way back as he sang 'I'm tired and I want to go to bed' he had run his hand along her upper leg, withdrawing it before she could protest and again giving her the complacent smile which this time acknowledged her complicity.

In an ideal marital relationship she would have discussed the matter with Michael, but she could not forecast his reaction and she did not want to risk another dining-room shuffle. Worst of all, he might just laugh. He had become quite unpredictable recently, light years removed from the young teacher whose selfless ambitions and liberal principles had seemed such a reproach to her own empty-headed young life. Somewhere along the way they had slipped past each other. As she became more and more involved in the serious business of being a responsible, civilized, concerned human being, Michael had drifted gradually from forecasts of radical upheaval to a kind of cynical materialist escapism which was as practically unprofitable for the Masson family as his earlier idealism had been for mankind at large. (Would she have minded so much, she sometimes asked herself, if he had turned into a successful capitalist?)

In the past year her concern about this change in him had reached new heights as his turning away from the high seriousness of life had become more marked. Always a *cinéaste*, he had seemed in the three years since he took up his lectureship to have accepted the world of the cinema screen on at least equal terms with reality. She had discussed his behaviour with various friends and even created models of possible behaviour patterns to present as case-histories to the psychotherapy group. Attempts to talk to Michael himself met with little response.

She moved uneasily. The sun was stinging her back.

'Michael,' she said.

He didn't answer so she dug her fingernails into his foot.

'Michael,' she said, raising her voice above the multi-lingual transistors. 'Is it time?'

'What? Oh Christ, I'm sorry. You should have turned ten minutes ago. I've been dreaming. Never mind. You'll be all right. Frozen meat's always the toughest.'

'What's that mean?' she snapped angrily, sitting upright and wriggling into a sun-top.

'Nothing really. Simply a reference to our cold and clammy native land. Time for our excursion, I think. Today I feel we can make it to Jugoslavia.'

'No, thanks,' she said, unmollified. 'I don't feel like it.'

'Not feel like it? Think of the welcome you'd get from

all those comrades who for four days now have been thronging the beaches of Croatia in daily anticipation of fraternal greetings from the Wesley Lane Labour Club.'

'No,' she repeated. 'And stop being elephantine.'

'You're not sick?' he asked. 'I felt a bit gippy last night myself.'

'Nothing like that,' said Sarah.

'You're sure? What about a Diocalm tablet washed down with an ice-cold lemonade? I'll go and get you one.'

She knew how much he hated joining the undisciplined mêlée round the beach bar and this evidence of solicitude soothed her irritation.

'No, honestly. You go and have a pedal by yourself. I'll just read my book. Go on, now. You never know what you'll pick up out there.'

'All right,' said Michael. 'I'll just try half an hour then.'

She watched him pick his way carefully through the recumbent bodies, past the *boule* players, down to the fat woman with the white yachting cap who was mistress of the pedal-boats. A few moments later, reclining in his canvas-backed chair like a bishop at the Athenaeum, he was heading out to sea.

'At last,' said Wilf, sitting down in the vacated deck chair, 'we are alone.'

Michael pedalled hard until he was well out of the inner band of bathers and boaters and only a couple of yachts broke the shimmering line where sky and sea met. He glanced back to the beach. It was a mere colourful ribbon, a long way away. Beneath him the water rocked gently with that hint of restrained power which great depth gives even on the calmest day. Michael was a poor swimmer but he had no fear in these conditions. Even the life-guard, who in choppier conditions would have been shepherding holiday-makers within fifty yards of the shore, was relaxing in the bottom of his boat.

Michael clambered out of his seat and lay on the small platform behind. The sun was a drug, he had decided. Ten minutes' exposure produced a mindless torpor in which the mind could cope with no concepts beyond the satisfaction of basic appetites. It was what he needed. Last year they had taken a cottage in North Wales and those damp winds and black simmering skies had opened up his mind to a torrent of past regrets and future fears which even whisky could not stem.

Now he could lie back and relax, quite untouchable. First, however, he prudently checked that the light breeze and tidal movement were drifting his craft inshore. He sometimes thought that the capacity to end his own life was the only real power left to him. But suicide as a fail-safe device was a Roman virtue; death by misadventure would be a silly little English farce.

He was awoken by someone grabbing his ankle and trying to pull him into the sea. Through his sun-shot mind ran thoughts of the dream he had invented to mock Molly with; then, as he plummeted closer to reality, of the boy in the red shirt mouthing threats through the coach window. Fully awake, he pulled his foot free of the questing hand and slithered as far from the platform edge as he could get.

'He's gone too far this time,' said Wendy.

She was hard to recognize. An elaborate bathing cap designed like a sunflower covered her hair, and the removal of her make-up by the sea made her appear at once younger and older. Her wrinkles were now visible but her skin looked healthy and he reduced the lower limit of her possible age by a couple of years.

'Would you like to come aboard?' asked Michael.

She was resting with her forearms on the platform and he thought she would need assistance if the rest of her substantial being was to be pulled out of the water. But she thrust herself upwards with surprising ease and he realized now what her appearance at this remove from the shore should have told him, that her bulk was not merely the flab of a chronic chocolate-box picker but the decay of a long-distance swimmer.

She was wearing a black one-piece swimsuit of rather severe cut. He watched with interest to see if she would take off her cap and reveal the true colour of her hair, but she merely shook her head so that the droplets of water fell off the sunflower like dewdrops, and settled down beside him.

'Give me a cigarette,' she said. He obeyed and lit one for himself, using a box of matches as he seemed to have mislaid his lighter. She drew in deeply.

'He's gone too far this time,' she said.

'Ah,' said Michael.

'It's come to blows. I knew it would.'

'Ah,' said Michael again.

'Yes. Look, why should you be involved? I'm sorry.'

Why indeed? thought Michael. It seemed to him a good cue for Wendy to leave, but she made no move. Perhaps it was expecting too much for her to plunge into the sea with half a cigarette in her mouth.

'You must be an excellent swimmer,' he said pleasantly.

'He's done it before, of course. But I told him last time. Just once more.'

'Yes. Well,' said Michael.

'What you see is the jolly surface. He's wild underneath. Mad. But he knows where to hit.'

'Look, Wendy,' said Michael, forced against his will to try to bring these obliquities on to the plane of a rational dialogue. 'Do you really want to talk about this? You hardly know me, after all, and while, if there's anything I can do in the name of common humanity, of course I'll do it, I can't just step into a family quarrel.'

That, he thought rather sadly, was an unacceptable offer of help if she'd ever heard one. This time she seemed to have taken the cue. She tossed her cigarette over the side and struggled into a kneeling position.

'Look,' she said.

She unfastened her left shoulder-strap and pulled the front of her bathing costume down, catching her heavy breast as she did so in a gesture which Michael mistook at first for modesty but which turned out to be merely manipulatory as she lifted it to reveal a dark bruise on the rib-cage beneath.

'Now do you believe me?' she said.

'My God!' exclaimed Michael, glancing anxiously

around to make sure he was the only witness.

Wendy took this as affirmation and fastened her strap again.

'We got married too young,' she said, moving to the edge of the boat and dangling her solid legs in the water.

'Always dangerous,' agreed Michael.

'I was a trainee nurse. Another two years and I'd have known better. Another fifty and he might have been ready for it.'

There was another long pause. Michael felt panicky. In his profession the temptation was always to break silences with questions and the only questions he could ask here would invite more confidences he didn't want.

'Can I give you a lift back to the beach?' he said in the end. There was enough of chivalry in this, he felt, to balance its finality.

'We'd better not let him see us together,' she said, and slid off the platform.

He examined this parting remark as he watched her swim away with a long slow stroke which would have drowned him had he attempted it. In the water he was like Sarah in her home life – only feverish activity kept him afloat. He wondered if he should tell her about this extraordinary interview. On the whole he thought not. Had these assertions of marital violence been offered direct to Sarah, she would not have rested till the whole squalid story was out, and not then. Even at second hand, the story would invite her total involvement, though she might have mixed feelings about the tit. Michael himself had mixed feelings about the tit.

He glanced at his watch. His time was nearly up.

That night he suggested they should skip the hotel dinner, take a bus into the old town and have a real Italian meal. To his surprise, Sarah, the family economist, agreed without demur. Rimini-città at night was a pleasant change from Rimini-marina. They strolled the whole length of the Corso d'Augusto, from the Bridge of Tiberius to the Arch of Augustus where the Via Flaminia began its journey to Rome. Not many people were around and as they stared up at the birds roosting on the ledges and capitals of the ancient arch, Michael felt safely distanced from the clutter of other people's lives at the Leonardo.

They had a meal in a restaurant at the edge of the Piazza Tre Martiri where the food was a distinct improvement on the hotel cuisine.

'Everything I see feels familiar in a dreamlike way,' said Michael. 'Even places that didn't appear in the film.'

'You mean *I Vitelloni*?'

'Yes. I'm sorry, did I ever take you to see it?'

'Only three times during the Fellini season at the film society a couple of years ago. I remember, though, you used to talk about it when we first met. All the time.'

'Did I? Well, it made a deep impression.'

'Deep perhaps, but not very firm,' observed Sarah drily.

'What?'

'You used to talk about its social comment. The death spasms of the bourgeoisie.'

'Did I say that? Ah well, what it was to be young and stupid. More wine?'

'Yes, please. I must admit it still looked like that to me when I saw it. These *vitelloni*, what were they? Just layabouts, surely? Empty lives. I mean, it was post-war Europe, wasn't it? Devoid of vitality or direction.'

'Balls.'

'That's what I mean. Your impression has changed. When I first met you, it was all social stuff. But then you started, I don't know . . .'

'So I grew out of *Bicycle Thieves*. But *I Vitelloni* is about, well, the avoidability of experience, you know, as if perhaps even in their failing, there's some hope. Not hope in any stupid political or even religious way, but as if unexpectedly out of something trivial . . . I'm not explaining this very well.'

'No,' said Sarah. 'You're not explaining it at all. Michael, sometimes what you say and do makes me wonder . . .'

'It's solutions that kill us. Isn't this veal splendid? Almost as good as you cook.'

'I never cook veal, you know that. It's inhuman.'

'Well, as good as your veal would be if you cared to cook veal.'

'Have you been up to something?' she asked. 'Or are you just changing the conversation?'

'What do you mean?'

'Compliments from you usually mean you've been up to something.'

He drank some more wine and laughed, though the observation was oddly disturbing. A flotilla of motor-scooters went by and he watched them through the open window as they wheeled round the Piazza. There were more than half a dozen of them, each with a young girl riding pillion. Michael's hang-ups were not specifically concerned with the fading of youth – indeed the memory of what he had been now set his teeth on edge – but there was something so utterly careless about the scooterists that he felt a pang of envy. Or perhaps it was love, like the Ancient Mariner and the water-snakes. Then a face among all those young faces turned in his direction and love and envy were both replaced by fear. It was the young man from the barbecue. He was sure of it. Even the shirt was the same.

Quickly he turned away from the window and downed the glass of Royal Stock which the waiter had just brought.

'What's up?' asked Sarah.

'Nothing. A tickle in the throat,' he said.

'Brandy won't help. Try some water.'

He hadn't told Sarah what had happened the previous night, any more than he had told her what had happened that afternoon. She was intensely curious about what he did when they were apart, but over the years had grown used to his uncommunicativeness. She had the habit of returning to topics and happenings long since divested of all interest for him, so he had developed a technique of silence which stood him in good stead when he really had something to hide. At the moment, of course, he did not really have anything to hide and he had a feeling that a frank and open discussion now might save a deal of trouble later on. But something in him shrank back from this kind of frankness and openness like a wary ant on the edge of a Venus' fly-trap.

The scooterists had more or less settled in a buzzing and still gently undulating swarm in front of an elegant neo-classical *tempietto* opposite the restaurant. Michael lingered over his brandy until Sarah pointed out that according to their calculations the last bus back to the sea-front was due in five minutes. They paid the bill and left. To reach the bus stop they had to walk diagonally across the square, passing within twenty yards of the young people. Michael resisted an impulse to hold a handkerchief to his face as if blowing his nose. There had been enough melodrama already.

As they reached the stop, the scooterists began to move again, not purposefully, but like birds in a field inexplicably disturbed, fluttering on high for a moment before settling to earth again.

There were two men at the bus stop already, one about fifty, the other much younger, early twenties at the most. They were both bearded, the young man with soft brown Christ-like wisps, while the older man resembled an English naval officer in a wartime movie. He wore blue-tinted sunglasses, a jacket that looked as if it had belonged to a City business suit, khaki drill slacks and tennis shoes. His companion wore a black tee-shirt, blue and white candy-striped flares, and no shoes at all. Round his neck on a silver chain was a tiny bell which tinkled as he moved. Between them stood a once-elegant hide suitcase and a large plastic carrier bag packed to explosion point.

'I hope we haven't missed it,' said Sarah. 'You never know with these Italian timetables.'

'Be comfortable,' said the naval officer. 'They are always a little late. Not much. Just enough to permit tardy passengers to catch their bus, not enough to irritate. Part of their amiable realism. You are English?'

'Yes,' said Sarah. Michael smiled warily and took a half-step sideways. Casual acquaintance he found a bore at the best of times; conversations at bus stops with unsavoury-looking men were fraught with danger.

'And you are staying at . . .?'

'The Leonardo,' said Sarah.

'I see. I see. A good hotel? I suppose, a *full* hotel?'

'Yes, I think it is. Full, I mean. It's not terribly good, though it isn't bad. Just an average package-deal place.'

'I see. Yes, the package. I am Sydney Dunkerley, by the way. My friend, Aristide. Forgive my curiosity, but we are between lodgings.'

His friend, Aristide, smiled nervously and rather ingratiatingly at the mention of his name. Dunkerley nodded reassuringly, though whom he was reassuring was not quite clear. He spoke English with an educated Home Counties accent, but as though he was used to speaking it with foreigners. Michael anticipated that Sarah would wish to know more about this being 'between lodgings'. In England a firm intervention at this point might have been necessary, but here there was no chance of her inviting them home. It was just a question of being bored till they got off the bus at the other end. He detached himself from the group and went to peer into a shop window. Reflected in the glass he saw the motor scooters wheel slowly by; all except one. It stopped and its rider stared towards Michael as though he had just discovered the Pacific, while the pretty girl on the pillion drew on a cigarette and yawned widely and smokily.

Hastily Michael rejoined the others. If the young Italian thought he had two male companions it might inhibit his thoughts of vengeance.

'. . . victims of circumstance,' Dunkerley was saying.

'But that's awful,' said Sarah. 'Where did you sleep?'

'Where all the dispossessed must sleep, my dear. On the beach. Not that we slept much. People patrol there all night. Not the *carabinieri*, fortunately, but lovers, hippies, and worse. You must take it in turn to watch your bags, of course. Somewhere close by someone was playing a Spanish guitar most abominably, never completing a phrase. There was very little sleep.'

'Are you on holiday?' enquired Michael, eager to establish his relationship with the group.

'In a manner of speaking,' said Dunkerley. 'Resting, to use a theatrical term. Between jobs.'

What else were they between? wondered Michael. He felt that, were he really interested in getting information, Aristide would be the better bet. He had not spoken but continually smiled and nodded whenever anyone else spoke. There was about him a kind of naïve eagerness to please which was rather attractive in a canine sort of way.

'Are you spending the whole season here?' enquired Dunkerely. 'Or will you move on?'

Sarah laughed, but Michael could see she was slightly flattered.

'Oh no,' she said. 'We're going to Venice for a few days, but then it's back to the grind.'

'Venice,' said Dunkerley. '*La Serenissima*. It has been so many years.'

'You know it?' said Sarah.

'Once intimately, now as a lovely memory. Perhaps I will go again. This summer for me is a time of revisitings. Old friends, places and people. Renewal. Yes, that's it.'

Cynically Michael wondered how many screams of horror would be choked back as doors were opened to reveal this face eager for renewal. Dunkerley struck him as a good man not to give your home address to, even if home was a thousand miles away.

The bus arrived. As it did so, the scooterist approached very slowly, moving just fast enough to avoid falling over.

'Signor!' he said. 'Hey, you! Inglese.'

The bus doors opened. Sarah was looking with interest at the Italian youth. Michael jumped athletically into the bus, then excused his rudeness by buying all four tickets at the barrier.

'Very kind,' said Dunkerley, who had gallantly assisted Sarah aboard.

'That boy, do you know him?' Sarah asked Michael.

'Who? Him? I don't think so. He's not one of the waiters, is he?'

'I don't think so.'

'An admirer, perhaps, madame,' said Dunkerley, leaning across the aisle. 'Creatures of sudden affections,

these young Italians, especially in the face of unusual
beauty.'

Sarah blushed and Michael observed her with dismay.
She looked pleased, indeed her expression was only a
short step away from a simper.

'It was me the boy seemed interested in,' he said
irascibly.

'Indeed,' said Dunkerley. 'My comment still holds, sir.
This is, after all, not Pall Mall.'

He settled back in his seat and began to talk rapidly
with Aristide in French. Michael's French was better
than his Italian but he could only pick out a few words. In
any case his mind was preoccupied with the boy in the
red shirt and he and Sarah didn't open their mouths till
the bus reached their destination.

It did not surprise him when the two men disembarked
at the same stop.

'Well, good night,' he said firmly, taking Sarah by the
arm.

'Good night indeed,' said Dunkerley. 'To hear the old
tongue spoken again and from such perfect lips makes
any night good.'

To hear anything other than English or German in the
streets of Rimini-Marina would be very difficult, thought
Michael.

'Perhaps I could be permitted to buy you a drink before
we part,' continued Dunkerley.

'Well, no thanks,' said Michael quickly. 'We'd better
get back to the hotel, it's been a long day. I'm quite worn
out.'

'But of course! A nightcap in the hotel bar, that's the
thing! Kill two birds.'

'But your lodgings,' protested Michael.

'Too late already, I fear,' said Dunkerley. 'As long as
we find a stretch of beach devoid of the Spanish guitar,
we'll be content, eh, Aristide?'

The youth smiled toothily and nodded.

'Yes,' said Sarah, 'that's a super idea. Let's have a
drink.'

She pulled herself free from Michael and with an

inviting smile to the naval officer and Jesus Christ, she set off towards the Leonardo.

Sarah was well aware of the irritation her actions were causing Michael. He was chronically suspicious of new acquaintances even when made in the most auspicious of circumstances. Even their closest friends still had the capacity to bore and infuriate him. Sarah on the other hand was a people-collector. Old ladies sat beside her on buses and told her their financial problems; young ladies buttonholed her in the supermarket queue and told her their sexual problems. Something in her face encouraged the stranger to speak, the troubled to seek sympathy, the guilt-ridden to confess. Among her many other social activities, she was on one night a week as a Samaritan, a good work which caused a serious rift between Michael and herself when early one morning, after listening sympathetically for more than a quarter of an hour to a tormented confession of incest, bestiality and wife murder, a stifled guffaw at the other end of the line told her all was not well. Michael later claimed drunkenness as excuse for his impersonation, but Sarah told him that what we do when the social reins slip shows what we really are.

But it was not just out of desire to irritate Michael, nor even for good humanitarian reasons that she was keen to keep the company of this strange couple. To tell the truth, she found them attractive. Not so much the older man, Dunkerley, who despite his bulk and naval beard rather reminded her of the Fox who in the film seduced Pinocchio with promises of an actor's life, but something about the younger man pressed the mothering button in her. He was, she gauged, an innocent abroad and in some danger, if not directly from the experienced Dunkerley (whose personal charm was undeniable and might even be sincere), then certainly from their association. Such impressions were difficult to communicate to Michael who had a nasty habit of recalling from the past one or two unfortunate instances of complete misinterpretation on her part. He might even have felt that she had got things wrong that afternoon if she had told him of her conversation with Wilf on the beach. She was not good at innuendo and it might be that she had misread Wilf's invitation to split a bottle of iced Asti Spumante in the cool of his bedroom.

'But your wife,' she had said, meaning *won't she mind being left on the beach*? Even as she spoke, the stupidity of her comment hit her.

'Yes,' Wilf had said. 'She's a problem, sure enough. She's out swimming at the moment. It's the only thing she's good at. Not much chance of her drowning, I'm afraid. But never worry, my dear. I'll think of something. Perhaps this evening.'

He had left shortly after and Sarah had been delighted when, as if by thought transference, Michael had suggested dining in town that night.

Michael had caught up with her and was walking along in a furious silence. She glanced over her shoulder and smiled encouragingly at the two men. About ten yards further back, weaving slowly from side to side of this relatively quiet side street, was a motor-scooter. She thought the rider might be the same boy who had spoken at the bus stop, but it was impossible to be sure. She contemplated mentioning the possibility to Michael as a truce offering, but decided against it. His behaviour was so childish that unconditional surrender was the only path to peace.

The bar was quite full. There were those who liked sitting up late drinking; and those who felt that on holiday they ought to sit up late, drinking; and those who wanted to go to bed but didn't think it was worth it because of the noise being made by the drinkers. The main source of noise was a juke-box built like a fairground steam-organ. The sound was deafening yet there seemed to be no shortage of willing hands to feed ten-lire pieces into it. The other source of noise was human voices shouting to be heard above the music.

'Well, well! Look who's here! Slimming, are we, or is our conversation too vulgar? Only joking! What are you drinking?'

It was of course Wilf, rising in a grotesque charade of old-fashioned courtesy from a large group of drinkers.

'No, thanks,' began Sarah, but Michael was too quick for her.

'That's kind of you, Wilf. Mine's a Campari-soda. We've brought a couple of friends along. OK if they join the gang?'

Sarah was angry but had to admire Michael. She spent a lot of time on committees trying to arrange people into the patterns which best promoted her purposes. She wasn't particularly good at it; other people's rights and feelings kept getting in the way. But she could appreciate the dexterity with which Michael had landed Wilf with a couple of extra thirsts to quench, diluted the presence of Dunkerley and Aristide by dropping them into a large pool of people, and, last but not least, taken revenge on her for inviting them here in the first place.

Sarah made the introductions, frostily refusing to acknowledge Wilf's quizzical glance as he took in the down-at-the-heelness of her two 'friends'. She sat on an old chintzy sofa which would have been at home in an English front parlour, with Dunkerley by her side and Aristide poised nervously on the edge of an adjacent chair.

Michael meanwhile had seated himself at some distance next to an amiable cockney couple who talked with the chirpy good humour of British film working classes before 1955. On his other side were Bob and Molly, but he preferred this situation to either sitting next to Wendy, who was hunched morosely at one end of a leather couch pushed slightly back from the group, or forming a new enclave with the two in-comers. He immediately set himself to being pleasant to those around him, most of whom he had earlier mocked ferociously from a distance. When he wanted to be nice, he did it well, Sarah had often observed. She sometimes felt like quoting his real opinions to the people he flattered, but immediately felt ashamed of her own resentment. Besides, he would ride the embarrassment so easily that it would be her oddity that was stressed, not his hypocrisy.

Wilf brought the drinks and settled down beside Sarah on the arm of the sofa.

'You staying nearby, Sydney?' he said over her head to

Dunkerley, who was making an Oliver Hardy business of tasting the Punt e Mes he had asked for.

'Yes, that is so. In a way.' Dunkerley smiled through his beard as he spoke, as though reassuring Sarah he would not cause her to lose face by admitting to his present vagrancy. Had he been concealing the fact for his own peace of mind, she would have co-operated readily, but she bridled at the assumption that she was worried by bourgeois prejudices.

'Sydney and Aristide are homeless at the moment,' she said in clear tones. 'They plan to spend tonight on the beach.'

Wilf nudged her knowingly and she realized he had of course spotted the baggage they had dumped in the foyer. His sharp little eyes wouldn't miss much.

'Have you known our lovely Sarah long, Sydney?' he asked next.

'We met only tonight. On an omnibus.'

'Well, well,' said Wilf. 'And it's the beach, is it? Well, you couldn't do it at Bognor.'

'Ah, Bognor Regis,' said Dunkerley like one sighing after the glory that was Greece. 'Bognor of the King.'

'Is that it? I always thought it meant Bognor where it piddles down! Where're you from then, Sydney?'

'Buckinghamshire,' said Dunkerley. 'Burnham. Do you know it? Burnham Beeches perhaps you've heard of?'

'Not what you'd call *know* it,' said Wilf. 'That's posh living, that place. Too rich for my purse.'

'There's some money about,' agreed Dunkerley. 'But it's mainly earned, I think you will find. The fruit of honest professional sweat.'

'Oh, no doubt. I don't doubt that at all. Very respectable place, Burnham Beeches. *Very* respectable. Tell you what, Sydney. I know what you are.'

'Oh?'

'Yes. You're one of those remittance men, I bet. No offence, but I bet if you turned up with your little bundle in the middle of Burnham Beeches, there'd be a few gracious ladies swooning away with shock.'

Sarah glared angrily at Wilf, who grinned back.

Dunkerley seemed unperturbed.

'I fear, Wilf (it is Wilf?), you overestimate both my female relatives' sensitivity and, I hope, my own repulsiveness.'

'Only joking, Sydney. Look, how about a fill-up? Sarah, you'll have another? And Napoleon here, he doesn't say much, does he?'

'Perhaps he hasn't heard anything worth answering yet,' snapped Sarah, sending Wilf into peals of laughter.

Aristide too smiled widely but vacantly, as though enjoying a joke he did not quite understand.

'Thank you,' he said in a voice so soft it was almost a whisper. 'I shall drink another Pernod, please.'

'Of course you shall, my love. And we'll all drink with you. Right then, who's empty? Come on, ladies, always drink when your hubbies drink. If it makes them active it might make you tolerant.'

'Oh for God's sake, shut up! You're the only *one* laughing. No one else finds you funny.'

It was of course Wendy who, having delivered this judgement, half rose and, leaning across three intervening bodies to Michael, said, 'Have you got a cigarette?'

Michael produced a packet, gave one to Wendy and lit it. She subsided, saying, 'Thank God there're still some gentlemen.'

The cockney couple were placidly disconcerted by the outburst. Bob looked at Michael with a mixture of dislike and puzzlement, flexing his deeply contoured arm muscles like a wrestler loosening up before a fight. To her surprise (she was not much given to prurient thoughts), Sarah found herself wondering what it felt like to have that huge weight of flesh and bone settling on top of your naked body. Molly didn't look strong enough. Perhaps they had come to some other arrangement.

Wilf dealt with Wendy by ignoring her, though Sarah noticed he was wise enough to buy her another drink. He was obviously a man who chose his victims carefully, always prodding and poking and ready to retreat with his jolly 'only joking!' at the first sign of counter-attack. Wendy was not a target to be aimed at in public, for the usual English sensitivity to *al fresco* unpleasantness was either missing or had been bludgeoned from her make-up. On the other hand, to ignore her occasional outbursts with a smile could win Wilf golden opinions from a casual observer. But he needed someone to make a butt of.

'Sydney, old son,' he resumed. 'So you're a gentleman of the roads, is that it? What we call back home, a tramp. Only joking! But why abroad, eh? What brings you to Europe. Tax avoidance?'

Dunkerley waited till Wilf's laughter had subsided.

'I like to combine business with pleasure,' he said.

'Well, the pleasure I can guess at, but what's your line of business?'

'I have many,' said Dunkerley. 'I know Italy well and have been useful to visitors. In recent years, I have captained charter yachts on the Med, managed a casino in North Africa and done a bit of soldiering further south.'

'Soldiering?' said Wilf. 'Shall we swing the lamp while you tell us a story? How I pommelled Rommel! Only joking!'

'Somewhat later than Rommel,' smiled Dunkerley.

'You mean you were a mercenary?' exclaimed Sarah.

'You could call it that.'

'In the Congo? One of those animals?'

'Among other places. In addition, talking of animals, I've done a bit of trapping for American zoos . . .'

'Hang about,' said Wilf. 'You mean you shot people? For money?'

'You make it sound like piece-work. But yes, that was my trade for a while.'

Dunkerley finished his drink and regarded Wilf steadily with a faint smile.

'I see,' said Wilf. 'Well, I've done a bit too.'

'National Service. Catterick,' said Wendy.

'Another drink,' said Wilf.

'I don't think . . .' said Dunkerley.

'One for the road!' said Wilf, rising.

Sarah glared indignantly at the bearded man and leaned across the arm of the sofa to address Aristide, thus forcing Wilf on his return to go round to Dunkerley's end.

'What do you do, Aristide?' she asked.

'Pardon?'

'What are you? Are you a student?'

'Yes. That is right. I am a student.' His thin features held an expression of sly humour for a moment.

'What do you study?' asked Sarah slowly.

'I came to Italy for seeing. Buildings, pictures, you understand?'

'I think so. You are an artist?'

'Yes. Artist.'

'And where are you studying? In France?'

He shrugged.

'Not study in France. My family is poor. *Paysans*. Working in country. You understand. I must live for me. Everything.'

'I see,' which she didn't, but what at least *was* clear was that beside her sat a genuine peasant boy, the unselfconscious incarnation of man's most basic driving forces, the class struggle and the pursuit of beauty.

The way in which the thought had formulated itself suddenly gave her pause. There was something ironical, almost mocking about it. For a moment she had felt her reaction to Aristide as Michael would most certainly feel it. Her appreciation of Bob as a problem in sexual logistics derived from the same source. It was intolerable that he should be tainting her mind like this!

She reached across and placed her hand over Aristide's. The boy was so surprised he nearly spilt his drink.

'I think that's splendid,' she said. 'Splendid.'

'I think that's splendid!' mimicked Michael as they got undressed for bed. 'What a lovely bit of Tory condescension. You really Thatchered that poor frog.'

'I thought you were too busy being smarmy to hear,' said Sarah. It was a vain game trying to keep cool and counterpunch, but it postponed the moment of explosive indignation which always left him looking insufferably self-satisfied, as though something had once again been proved.

'My dear,' he said. 'The English Tory lady's voice was

designed to echo round the world, didn't you know?
What do you mean, *smarmy*?'

'You don't like those people, do you? You just went out
of your way to be pleasant to them to put Aristide and
Sydney out in the cold.'

He didn't deny it, but grinned.

'Life,' he said, 'is a series of clubs which every day we
apply to, become members of, or are blackballed from.
For me, tonight was a joining night. Syd and Ari, they
applied but, well, you've got to be careful who you
admit. Let one in, you know, and they'll take over. But
it was your friend Wilf who dropped in the blackballs,
not me.'

'He's not my friend!'

'He imagines he is. There's a kind of conspiratorial smirk
which comes over his face whenever he addresses you.'

'Is this a jealous scene?'

'Why no,' he said. 'It's a frank exchange of trivia,
with a bit of sound and fury thrown in, like late-night
chat shows, union meetings, academic boards, and
parliaments. Signifying nothing.'

'Oh God, Michael,' she said. 'Something terrible's
happened to you since we got married.'

'No,' he said. 'Nothing terrible, that's the point. My
life has been a rose-strewn path. Perhaps I am moving
along an arc from vicarious indignation at the horror of
life to genuine gratitude for the deliciousness of life, and
have so far only progressed to a mild, uncentred discontent.
Bear with me a few years and you shall see me a grinning
optimist yet.'

He stumbled as he tried to pull on his pyjama trousers.
His mouth was bitter with the aftertaste of half a dozen
Campari-sodas. Like lust, they were a bliss in proof, and
proved a very woe.

He went into the bathroom and cleaned his teeth,
returning to take up the cudgels again, but Sarah was in
bed with her face pressed firmly into the pillow.

'Lights out, is it?' he said. 'Perhaps as well.'

But even this provoked no response and he too climbed
into bed.

The banging on the wall finally woke him, though the noise of upraised voices had woven itself into the pattern of his dreams some minutes earlier.

It was hard to say whether the banging was communicative or merely incidental to some other activity. Beside him Sarah stirred but did not waken. Their roles had been oddly reversed. Or perhaps not so oddly. It had always been an unconscious technique of hers to seek out others to share a burden of concern or distress, and a little while later (to continue the metaphor) she would suddenly stoop to grasp another load, leaving the first firmly wedged on her confidant's shoulders.

The row next door continued. Michael climbed out of bed, picked up his cigarettes and matches and went out on the balcony, partly to spare Sarah the smell of tobacco on the bedroom air and partly because he'd be better placed to hear his neighbour's dialogue.

A climax had been reached.

'You're vile!' screamed Wendy. 'Vile! Sex, sex, sex, that's all. Sex, sex!'

'What do you know about sex?' demanded Wilf, his voice high with rage. 'What the *hell* do you know about anything? You useless bitch!'

'That Jackie! Who'd be a mother?'

'Not you for one. What Jackie?'

'Oh come on!' Wendy laughed stridently. '*That* Jackie! The one who left the shop. Sixteen. God, I often think about her mother!'

Michael lit his cigarette, leaned on the towel-draped metal rail which ran round the balcony, and admired the night sky and Wendy's skill in dispute.

Wilf's rage had been temporarily diluted by honest bewilderment.

'Whose mother?' he asked.

'Don't imagine everyone didn't know why she asked for her cards after just a fortnight. You've been a dirty byword for years. Jennifer.'

'Who?'

'Jennifer was her name.'

'Oh God! You mean Gillian? That was five years ago!'

'Jesus Christ! What is this? Some kind of anniversary?'
'And what about her mother?'
'What are you trying to tell me?' screamed Wendy. 'You had a go at her mother as well, is that it?'
'I didn't know her mother,' roared Wilf. 'You stupid cow, I never mentioned her mother!'
'No, you wouldn't! You wouldn't! That's typical. Get your hands on anything, that's you. Well, I'm tired of it, tired of it. This is the end. Ah! Don't you touch me! Keep off!'

There was the sound of energetic activity, the patter of feet, some thuds and grunts of the kind one associates with a boxing match on radio, one last high yelp followed by the opening and slamming of a door, a moment's silence, then a steady regular sobbing.

Michael placed his cigarette carefully on the rail and leaned out towards the neighbouring balcony which was about four feet away, trying to see into the room.

The sobbing continued, and with it a scratching, scuffling noise as though someone were trying to crawl across the floor.

'Wendy,' he called in a low voice.

There was no reply.

'Wendy!' he called a little louder.

There was a pause in the crawling noise.

'Oh help,' came a faint cry.

He saw a mental picture of the bedroom next door, the furniture in disarray, the woman battered – perhaps bloodstained – trying to crawl to the door. This was the time for a man of action to act.

'Oh shit,' he groaned. And pulled himself up on to the balcony rail.

Instantly he knew he had made a mistake. The four-foot gap was at least six foot, probably more. Steve McQueen would need to pay a stuntman thousands of dollars to take that step. He clutched at the wall for support, adjusted his standing on the rail prior to descent, and trod on his burning cigarette.

Michael went forward. He flung out his arms, opened his mouth to shriek and felt all the breath knocked out of his body as he folded up across the rail of the neighbouring balcony.

The pain was agonizing. He felt sure the wall of his stomach must have burst open. When he slithered over to the safety of the balcony itself he sat for a while with his hands pressed to his belly, convinced that he could feel a hot stickiness oozing through his fingers. After a while he was brave enough to hold one hand up into the ray of light falling through the open window. There was no trace of blood. His injuries then must be internal. He remembered his Western lore. Drink no water with a stomach wound. Perhaps Wilf had some whisky. Slowly he rose and stepped into the bedroom.

Wendy lay outstretched on the floor. For a moment his own pains were forgotten. With difficulty she raised her head.

'Have you got a cigarette?' she asked. 'Mine have got knocked under the bed somewhere.'

He shook his head and she stood up. She was wearing a white nylon nightdress saved only from complete transparency by outcrops of lace. There was a faint discoloration on her left cheek which may have been the result of a blow, but it was her hair which held his attention. The gipsy wig adorned a bust on the dressing-table. It was flanked by two others in different styles but equally black. But Wendy's real hair was a rich red, cut very short now but with promise of growing to fall in voluptuously undulating tresses.

'Why on earth do you wear a wig?' he asked. It was a non sequitur worthy of Wendy herself.

'Disguise,' she said. 'Have you got belly-ache?'

Indeed he had. He looked down and along the line of his pyjama cord a dark red weal was visibly uprising. He pulled his pyjamas up to cover it and winced.

'I hit the rail,' he said. 'Look, are you all right?'

'Me. Oh yes. The usual. He's not the puncher he was. It's all this sex and drinking.'

She turned and began opening drawers. As she bent forward, her haunches swelled magnificently towards him.

'But your face . . .'

'I did that. He was making a gesture, you know, like Hitler. He's a lot like Hitler. I walked into it.'

'Where's he gone now?'

'God knows. He'll find someone to pour his woes out to and his spunk into. Here it is. Lie down.'

She turned and came towards Michael with a tube of ointment in her hand.

'What?' he said, alarmed.

She pushed him back on the bed, flipped open his pyjama pants, squeezed some white oily substance on to his belly and began to rub it into the weal.

'I used to be a nurse,' she said. 'That's where we met. He was in for his appendix. He got an erection when they were shaving him, can you believe that? I should have been warned, but I was young. It's a pity they didn't chop it off.'

'Yes,' he said. 'Yes.'

What is wrong with this picture? he asked himself. He had come to help a woman in distress and instead he was lying on his back in a state of increasing bliss with his pants around his bum while her strong fingers rubbed his belly.

I mustn't get an erection, he thought in alarm. Not after what he had just heard. She wouldn't make the same mistake twice.

'Why don't you get a divorce?' he asked.

'Divorce? I don't know. Why doesn't everybody? Why don't you?'

'Me? Well, why, God, I don't beat my wife for one thing.'

'She's a bit serious, isn't she? That's nice. I like a serious woman.'

She squeezed out some more ointment and brought both hands to bear on the job. Michael realized he was fighting a losing battle. Her apparent obliviousness of any possible sexual reaction to her first aid only made things worse. It was time to go.

There was a knock at the door.

'Come in,' called Wendy.

The door opened. There stood Bob in a tartan robe. Only a slight widening of the eyes disturbed his impassive expression as he took in the scene before him.

'We heard a noise,' he said. 'Then quiet. Molly said I should come.'

'Thanks. That's kind of you. Everyone's very kind,' said Wendy. 'What do you think of divorce, Bob?'

'Me? I don't. Well, if you're all right . . .'

'Sure, Bob. Thanks a lot. Tell Molly thanks, but there's nothing to be done. Unless I kill the bastard.'

'Good night then,' said Bob, retreating.

The intrusion had been like a douche of cold water to Michael's incipient passion, but it was still time to go.

He sat upright, pushing Wendy gently aside.

'Thanks,' he said. 'That's helped a lot. You'll be all right now? If you want anything, we're just next door. All right?'

'I sometimes wish I was back in the hospital,' she said. 'There'd be something there I could give him to send him off.'

'I'd see a solicitor,' he advised.

'I did once. He tried to put his hand up my skirt. No, you're on your own in the end, don't you agree?'

She looked at him with that curiously blank gaze which was probably due to some sight deficiency but which made him feel that a glass partition stood between them; though who was in the tank and who was looking in was impossible to say.

He smiled weakly, opened the door and, after checking that the corridor was empty, he left. Sarah was still asleep. He wondered if she'd taken one of her sleeping tablets. After sitting on the lavatory with a cigarette for five minutes, he took one himself.

III

Next morning they slept in and missed breakfast. The sun was shining, but the sea was running up the sandy beach with unusual ferocity reminding Michael of the beach scene in *I Vitelloni*, and far out along the horizon stretched a line of cloud as dark and as deadly as an artillery barrage.

The sunbathers were there in their customary crowds, but now the beach attendants were moving among them, folding down the parasols and stacking the deck chairs.

'At a guess,' said Michael, 'I would say those fellows know something we don't.'

The storm, or rather the edge of it, arrived fifteen minutes later. There was no rain, but the wind caught and clawed at everything loose, sending streamers of sand into the air and cracking the hotel flags like a line of bullwhips on their arching cords. The storm centre remained at sea and distant lightnings sent their delayed thunders rumbling shorewards on the wind.

Michael and Sarah sat in the lounge at a sea-facing window, watching with interest the last few hardy Englishmen who refused to believe such weather was permitted on the Adriatic.

'A splendid sight,' said a cultured voice behind them. 'Home thoughts from abroad.'

They looked round. Dunkerley beamed down at them. In his arms he carried a young girl whom they recognized as one of the large family belonging to the tour company courier, a pleasant but inefficient woman who clearly knew where an Italian mother's loyalty lay. Her technique for dealing with queries and complaints was to take copious notes and do nothing. She approached Dunkerley now, who greeted her like an old friend and passed over the child with shows of great reluctance on both sides. The mother looked delighted at the praise Dunkerley was obviously showering on the girl and allowed her to accept a fifty-lire piece from the fat man.

Aristide appeared now as if the disappearance of the child was his cue. He smiled shyly.

'May I join you?' said Dunkerley, sinking into an armchair.

'Aristide, come and sit here,' said Sarah, patting the arm of her chair. 'Michael, what about some coffee?'

Michael scowled but rose obediently and went out of the lounge to the bar. The alleged waiter service never worked and there was a large crowd waiting for coffee. It would have been a queue but for the anarchic presence of a handful of Italians and Germans. He gritted his teeth and began to worm his way forward.

'Who're you pushing? Wait your bloody turn.'

It was the male half of the amiable cockney couple, not so amiable now.

'Sorry,' said Michael.

'It's bad enough with these buggers. Beat them in two world wars and they still want to fight!'

'Make way, oh, make way,' said Wilf, who was leaning on the bar. 'This man needs sustenance. No dinner, no breakfast, Mike? What are you living on, the fruits of love? Do me another two cappuccinos, Mario.'

He looked fit, well-rested, and full of gaiety. How it was possible to sail so serenely through those nightly marital storms Michael could not imagine.

'No, I'll get them,' he said. 'There are four of us.'

'Four,' repeated Wilf. 'My overdraft will stand it. Another two, Mario.'

'It's Dunkerley and his friend,' Michael felt obliged to point out. His belief that the Wilfs of life should be made to pay for their existence had not changed, but even he had felt slightly shamed when the two visitors had drunk their way through six or seven rounds without even a feint towards their pockets.

'Who? Oh, Syd and Arry. Fine, fine. Interesting pair. I like to meet a variety of people. Thanks, Mario. Careful with the chocolate, I likes my cocoa at night. Now, listen, Mike, isn't this weather bloody awful? There's nothing to do in this place except booze and play cards. So I thought, what about a drive? Hire a car, packed lunch, out into the highways and byways. See a bit of the real Italy. Tread a few grapes, squeeze a few peasants. Are you on?'

'It's a bit short notice,' parried Michael. 'I doubt if you'll get a car now.'

'Oh, I've got the car. You're right in a way, though. Lots of people had the same idea, and all the smaller cars had gone. I've got a bloody great Fiat, expensive but you can take six comfortably and spread the cost.'

'I see,' said Michael. 'It's my money not my company you're after.'

But he said it with a smile to show he was joking. The truth was that he and Sarah had contemplated hiring a car to do some inland exploring but the cost had made them think again. Their budget was, if not tight, certainly close-fitting, and such luxuries as hire-cars were not to be undertaken lightly. Sarah had examined the facts and voted against on economic grounds, cleverly concealing (from herself also, in some degree) the true cause of her dissent, which was Michael's driving. She did not drive herself and was an atrocious passenger, in constant fear of death or disablement. Michael's casual, undisciplined driving style was a source of daily terror at home. Here among these crazy Italians it must destroy them both.

Michael let himself be dissuaded with a display of irritation which concealed (though not from himself) his great relief at not having to drive in Italy.

But to see a bit of the countryside would be nice. The question was, could having one's own car begin to compensate for a day in the company of Wilf and Wendy? He doubted it.

'Darling,' he said. 'Here's Wilf with coffee and a proposition.'

Wilf nodded amiably at Dunkerley and outlined his plan to Sarah.

'Who else is going?' asked Michael.

'Well, just the three of us so far,' said Wilf. 'Bob and Molly and me. Wendy doesn't fancy it. Gets car sick. A delicate tummy.'

'Ah,' said Michael. The absence of Wendy more than compensated for the presence of Bob, he felt.

'So we'd make five,' he said. 'Still a place.'

'May I venture to volunteer myself?' said Dunkerley, who had already downed his coffee. 'If it is not a private and esoteric party, perhaps I could be of some assistance. I'm well acquainted with the neighbouring countryside, speak the language fluently and feel I might be of some use in ensuring that no pleasure is missed.'

To Michael's surprise, Wilf did not crush this suggestion with the rude guffaw he expected. True, they had ended up on better terms the previous evening than the opening salvos had promised. Dunkerley's revelation of his African activities had lost him Sarah's auspices but seemed favourably to impress Wilf. Still, at the very least Michael expected an enquiry to be made as to whether Dunkerley was proposing himself as a paying passenger or a paid guide.

'Include me out,' interrupted Sarah.

'Oh no. Tragic!' exclaimed Wilf.

'Like Wendy, I've a weak stomach,' said Sarah. 'Michael, dear, you go, please. I know you're keen to see the Malatesta castle where Francesca was killed.'

'Who?' said Wilf.

'Francesca da Rimini,' said Dunkerley. 'Wife of Gianciotto Malatesta who, having surprised her in the arms of his brother, Paolo, stabbed them both to death.'

'Quite right too,' said Wilf. 'It's a husband's privilege. What say you, Bob?'

Bob turned from the nearby group he was talking with and said, 'What's that?'

'Deceived husband should have the right to chop his wife's boy-friend. It's a story Syd here's been telling us. Good man to have along on our little trip, I'd say. He knows all the local filth. Right then, Mike. Half an hour, shall we say? At the front of the hotel. Will you pick up the packed lunches? See you!'

'Well, this is nice,' said Dunkerley, stretching himself luxuriantly in his armchair. 'I've some small experience of being a courier, of course. Mainly in South America and the African game reserves.'

'I suppose it doesn't pay as well as shooting people,' said Sarah acidly.

'True. But at least the people you work with aren't shooting back.'

'Don't be too sure,' said Michael gloomily. Dunkerley obviously thought of himself as a non-paying passenger, which left only three men to divide the expenses unless Wilf found someone to fill the sixth place.

'You know,' he said to Sarah, 'if you're not going, I don't think I'll bother either.'

She looked at him, surprised.

'Don't be stupid,' she said.

'But what will you do?' he asked.

'Darling, even with your non-productive, layabout job, we spend more than half of our lives away from each other. If you must have a timetable, I shall do some present-shopping and finish *The Gulag Archipelago*.'

She glowered at him as she spoke. Strange, he thought, how her resentment at any suggestion of dependence on his company never inhibited her keen desire to know where he had been.

'All right, I'll go.'

'Splendid,' said Dunkerley. 'I have just been planning an itinerary in my mind and you would be foolish to miss it. Sarah, my dear, do not worry if we are not back by dinner-time. I shall return him to you by midnight.'

'As late as that, Mr Dunkerley? Take a wooll Michael, just in case.'

'Don't let Aristide get under your feet. He has things do such as searching out some accommodation for us.'

He spoke sharply to Aristide in French and the boy nodded and smiled.

'If he might be permitted to leave our luggage in your room, it would be a great help,' said Dunkerley. 'It's heavy to carry and dangerous to leave, even in the foyer of so illustrious an hotel.'

'Of course,' said Sarah.

'Splendid. Then come along, Michael. There are these

packed lunches to collect, are there not?'

Sarah watched them go, entertained by Dunkerley's
emergence as the organizer of the trip. Michael's need
to be persuaded into doing the things he wanted had long
ceased to entertain her. She turned to Aristide and
received the usual white-toothed smile. He looked much
fresher this morning, having changed into a rather smart,
dark brown sports shirt and put a pair of green plastic
sandals on his feet.

'Tell me,' she said, 'how did you first meet Mr Dunkerley?'

She had discovered that if she spoke slowly, slightly
exaggerating her mouth movements as though to a deaf
lip-reader, he picked up nearly everything she said.

'We meet in Marseilles. He was very helping to me.
There was a trouble and he helped.'

'Oh. What kind of trouble? With the police?'

'No. Not police.'

Aristide looked slightly put out and Sarah smiled
apologetically.

'No,' he continued. 'With, I do not know the word.
Not police, but uniform, yes.'

'Bus conductors? Soldiers?' she suggested.

'No. In the prison. Guardians. Trouble with guardians.'

'Prison guards? Warders?' said Sarah.

'Guard-warders, yes.'

'You were in prison? Both of you? What for? What
crimes had you and Mr Dunkerley committed?'

'Ah. Crimes. Yes. Different crimes. Stealing. In supermarket, food tins. Like in America, rip-off. You understand rip-off?'

Sarah nodded. She felt considerable theoretical sympathy for the rip-off philosophy and in addition had
written letters to the local press about the temptation to
crime presented by supermarket sales techniques.

'And Mr Dunkerley?'

'Yes, Mr Dunkerley.'

'The other crime,' she said slowly. 'What was that?'

'Ah,' he shrugged. 'Not good. A girl. Pff!'

He made a breathy whistling noise and flicked his forefinger across his cheek.

'A girl? I'm sorry, what . . .?' said Sarah.

'Girl. *Putain.* Jig-a-jig girl. She tries to keep too many money. Not pay her share. So, pff!'

'My God!'

Well, it fitted, she thought. Dunkerley the pimp, razor-slashing young prostitutes who wouldn't pay.

'But he helped you in prison.'

'Yes, helping,' said Aristide, nodding vigorously.

'What happened?'

'Guard-warder who likes me, he wants . . . wait, I have learnt the word . . . he wants to bugger me. Yes. Bugger me.'

Despite the strongest effort of her will, Sarah's head moved round to check the reactions of those who sat near them in the now crowded lounge. On one side were an elderly retired couple, so precisely on the mid-point of the curve which runs from the unselfconscious raucousness of the working class to the self-congratulatory braying of the upper that in public they never addressed each other above a whisper. Though they sat trancelike now, one staring at the window, the other at the wall, their heads were cocked like robins' and Sarah almost preferred the undisguised attentiveness of the coarse-featured woman in curlers on the other side.

'I think I should like a walk,' she said. 'A *walk*. Will you come?'

'Yes. Walk,' agreed Aristide, rising and following her from the lounge. In the foyer he bent behind a table and rose up with the old suitcase and stuffed carrier bag.

'I'd forgotten those,' said Sarah. 'Hang on.'

She went to the reception desk and claimed her key and then, followed by the curious gaze of the receptionist, she led Aristide up the stairs.

The cleaners were in her room, two placidly jolly women who did what they felt essential with calm efficiency and neglected the rest with equally calm indifference. Sarah tried to see in them nothing but the dignity of labour to counterbalance Michael's judgement that Latin layabouts were even worse than their English counterparts; but unemptied ashtrays and untucked-in sheets were a constant irritation.

They smiled at her in greeting as she came through the door then more broadly at each other when Aristide followed her.

'Put them down there and push them under the bed,' ordered Sarah.

Aristide obeyed, one of the women spoke and they both laughed, hesitating a moment when Aristide uttered a few words of rapid Italian, then all three laughing loudly together.

'What was the joke?' asked Sarah casually as they descended the stairs.

'Joke?'

'Yes. Why did you laugh?' she said slowly.

'Ah, the women. She ask the other, shall we fetch another bed? And I say, no thanks, one will do all three.'

He laughed again and Sarah smiled uncertainly. She did not care for suggestive conversations, but after all, she had asked Aristide what had been said.

Outside there were still quite a lot of people walking aimlessly along the beach. The air was warm by British standards, despite the wind which ran the breakers up the easy shore as though in a failure-doomed effort to lick the coastline clean of concrete and glass, metal and plastic. Sarah tried to balance in her mind the employment opportunities offered by the building and running of this vast holiday machine against its empty-headed and non-productive function. All this money. If you stopped and listened carefully you could almost hear it chinking into the tills above the gusty wind.

Surprised by such imaginative thoughts, she glanced at Aristide as though he might be laughing at her and saw that the tinkling sound she heard derived from the wind-swung bell charm he wore round his neck.

'What do you do for money?' she said. 'How do you earn money?'

'Money,' he said, making a gesture of the left shoulder which may have been contempt or bewilderment. 'Sydney makes money. Sometime I work, in farm or in shop, but not long. Sometime beg. Sometime steal. Watch.'

He did a slow mime, approaching a beach table on which a single plastic cup had resisted the pressures of the wind. Twice he circumambulated the table, moving closer each time. Then he swayed slightly as though on some unevenness of the sand and the cup was gone. He returned to Sarah smiling expectantly, and when he reached her pulled the cup from beneath his vest and offered it.

The whole action filled Sarah with unease, not because of its morality which she was always willing to debate in terms of social and psychological cause and effect, but because during it Aristide, without shedding one whit of his charming lost-puppy-dog appeal, had appeared so purposeful, even dangerous. Now the young dog was back, offering its stick, eager for applause.

'That is wicked,' she reproved sternly.

'I know,' he said, still grinning. 'Only joke. Sometime a peach. Nothing more.'

She wasn't sure whether she believed him and they walked on through a grove of beach-umbrellas which, folded down, shook like dead Christmas trees in the turbulent air.

'How does Mr Dunkerley, Sydney, make his money?' she asked.

'Many ways,' said Aristide mysteriously. 'See, here we sleep last night.'

He took her arm and led her to a row of beached pedal-boats.

'In a boat?' asked Sarah.

'No. Too hard. On the sand.'

He pointed to where between two boats could be seen a shallow hollow not yet filled in by the wind.

'It is soft. Here. You try.'

Still holding her arm he sank down and she sank with him.

The texture of the sand appeared no different from that on which she and half a million others sunned themselves every day, but Aristide seemed to expect some comment.

'Very nice,' she said.

She wanted to stand up, but he had such a tight grip on her arm just above the elbow that it was impossible without forcibly prying herself loose. For a cold moment she feared he was making some kind of pass at her, but now he stood upright, helped her to her feet and waved her courteously out of the space between the boats as though ushering her into a drawing-room.

After half a mile Sarah tired of the wind and the energy-sapping sand and suggested they turned into the town. Aristide agreed readily – it was *very* like taking a dog for a walk, she thought again. They stopped for a drink when they reached the main street, which the weather had rendered unusually crowded with tourists for this time of day.

Sarah drank her cappuccino and watched Aristide excavate the huge ice-cream confection he had chosen. It struck her that this was perhaps all he had eaten that morning, but she was a little reassured by the thought that Dunkerley did not seem the type to tolerate such fasting.

Aristide looked up suddenly and caught her watching him. He smiled. A smear of pink and green ice-cream ran like theatrical make-up along his bottom lip.

'You nice lady,' he said. 'Kind. Like my mother.'

Was he mocking her? Please to God let him be mocking her! Sarah in her mind heard quite clearly Michael's laughter at the scene. Would she ever tell him? She had told him too much in the past and knew now that a deflation shared was usually at some time in the future a deflation repeated.

'Tell me about your mother,' she said brightly.

'Poor family,' he said. 'My father he cut wood. You know, chop-chop.'

He made axe-swinging motions.

'Much drink,' he went on. 'My mother, no drink. Much pray, much sorrow. My father beat her. Beat me. Beat my brothers, sisters. Beat all.'

He was silent for a moment, looking more serious, older, than she had yet seen him.

'I grow,' he said. 'One day, I beat him. Then I come away.'

'But how terrible!' cried Sarah, wishing she didn't really feel 'how marvellous!' 'But you are in touch? Do you write? Do you send letters home to your mother?'

He shrugged. 'She not read very well. Some day I go home. Next year, year after. Maybe.'

Sarah paid the bill and they left. It did cross her mind that Aristide could be a rather expensive friend but immediately, as if sensing her thought, he touched her shoulder lightly and disappeared into a souvenir shop, returning a few moments later with a small paper bag which he presented to her. She opened it and took from it a necklet, a small enamelled medallion on a fine chain.

'Thank you, Aristide,' she said. 'It's lovely. You shouldn't have. It's too much.'

'Yes,' he agreed. 'Buy, no steal.'

He grinned as he spoke and she smiled back, a fully shared joke.

When they got back to the hotel, to Sarah's surprise the first person she saw was Molly.

'Hello,' she said, approaching. 'What's happened to the expedition?'

'They've gone,' said Molly. She was sitting at a table outside the town entrance to the hotel, writing postcards. Sarah glanced uncertainly over her shoulder at Aristide. She did not wish to appear rude but it looked like a good chance to talk with Molly, whose shyness always seemed worse in the presence of men. And in addition she wanted to know the whys and wherefores of this suddenly all-male expedition.

Aristide waved his hand as though reading the situation.

'Go now and look at lodging,' he said. 'Later, I come once more. Ciao!'

He really was a pleasant boy, thought Sarah. And interesting too.

Settling down beside Molly, she said rather more forcibly than intended, 'And why haven't you gone with them?'

'Well, I thought, when Bob said that Wilf said you

weren't going, and not Wendy either . . .'

She tailed off. Sarah felt absurdly guilty.

'Oh, I'm sorry. I never thought. I've spoilt your day.'

Molly didn't deny it but nervously shuffled her post-cards. She was a pretty girl, in her early twenties, Sarah guessed, five or six years younger than her husband, perhaps the youngest woman in his social circle and always very conscious of this. Sarah had not been able to dig out much background material so far but she had a picture of Molly trapped in some council semi surrounded by working women or older wives whose lives were kids and curlers. Though the council semi might be wrong. Without knowing what Bob did, it was impossible to say. That was a mystery that now seemed a good time to solve.

'Mind you,' said Sarah, 'I didn't much fancy being stuck in a car all day on a culture tour. It'll be red hot inland. Bob likes that kind of thing, does he?'

Molly stared at her uncomprehendingly. Really, Aristide was easier going.

'Frescoes, churches, Roman ruins. Is Bob interested in that?'

'No,' said Molly. 'I don't think so. Is that what they're doing?'

She sounded quite incredulous and Sarah felt an odd pang of unease. Stag groups had always bothered her and in recent years she had surprised herself as well as Michael by the vehemence with which she had opposed the traditional all-male pint when friends had visited them for lunch. Casseroles had proved the answer. Now everyone went to the local while her mother looked after the children. She would have looked after the cooking too, but Sarah felt almost as strongly about this.

'I assumed so,' she said. 'What else is there for them to do?'

'I don't know,' said Molly, wrinkling her brow. Did she imagine they'd gone off for a pint of bitter followed by a football match? wondered Sarah.

'Bob's not a culture vulture then,' she said.

'Oh no.'

'Well, I suppose it's more in Michael's line. He's in education, you know. A lecturer,' she enunciated carefully.

'Yes, I know.'

'And Bob?'

'Yes?'

'What's his line?'

'He's not a lecturer. No,' said Molly. 'Is it lunchtime yet?'

'Hardly,' said Sarah. 'It's only quarter past eleven.'

'Is that all?' said Molly. 'I wonder what they are doing now?'

'Yes,' said Sarah. 'I wonder.'

'But it tastes pretty awful,' said Michael.

'Balls! Add a pint of port to one of these and you've got something lethal. Lethal, I tell you. Your original sexual fire-water. It dissolves knickers, this stuff.'

Wilf held up one of the half-dozen litre bottles of San Marino brandy he had just purchased.

'Now give us a hand and we'll get them to the car. Two each. There we go.'

He doled them out to Bob and Michael. Dunkerley was some distance away talking intimately to the store proprietor; probably bargaining over commission, thought Michael. He felt extremely disgruntled. A morning in San Marino in search of cheap liquor was not his idea of a profitable use of the car. Not that San Marino, with its Disney adventure-film fortresses perched on precipitous bluffs, was not worth visiting. But it was packed full of tourists brought by the coachload from all along the Adriatic. The Leonardo itself seemed very well represented and Wilf halted from time to time to exchange greetings.

Back at the car, they stacked the bottles in the boot and opened the doors to air the interior. Here, over twenty kilometres inland, the disturbed coastal weather was only a distant haze and the sun turned parked cars into ovens. Wilf had got their Fiat into the shadow of a motor-coach, but even so it was unpleasantly warm.

'Shall we be off?' asked Wilf. 'I can see you're ready

for it, Mike. OK, Bob? Hey, Syd, over here! God, look at him sweat!'

Dunkerley joined them, mopping his brow with a rough cotton square which looked like the last infirmity of a shirt.

'Where now?' demanded Wilf. 'Mike here wants peace and peasants, the real thing, not this tourist junk.'

He spoke indignantly as though blaming Dunkerley for having brought them here.

'His wish, my command,' said Dunkerley gravely.

'Then let's get some speed up and cool down,' said Wilf.

Following Dunkerley's directions, they sped westwards out of San Marino. Michael settled back to enjoy the ride. From time to time he wished they could stop and take a closer look at the countryside they passed through, but he felt that in a sense, having got his own way already, it would be inequable to request further concessions. When he saw what their destination was, he was glad he hadn't. Sansepolcro. Dunkerley had done him well.

Wilf brought the car to a halt with a flourish of brakes that would not have disgraced a native.

'Gentlemen,' the fat man said, gesturing circumambiently, 'Sansepolcro.'

Bob stared out at the old and rather dilapidated red-roofed buildings which surrounded them.

'Looks a bit of a dump.'

'It is the birthplace of Piero della Francesca,' said Dunkerley, shocked. 'Here you may see what Aldous Huxley described as the greatest painting in the world, Piero's "Resurrection".'

'I'd rather have a bite to eat.'

Bob was the only one who claimed an appetite and the others settled for huge glasses of beer to wash the heat of the car ride away while he worked his way through the packed lunches.

Michael rose fairly quickly to do some exploring. To his annoyance Wilf finished his drink and came after him.

'Feeling happier, now, Mike?' he said genially, falling into step alongside.

'Yes, thanks,' said Michael.

'Good. Something for everyone, that's the ticket. Nice, this place, not a lot of life, but nice all the same. Tell me, Mike, you're an educated man, been around a bit, what do you make of Syd?'

'I'm sorry?'

'Is he for real, do you think? I mean, all this from Eton to the Congo stuff. Or is he just a bum?'

'Well,' said Michael, 'he sounds like a semi-educated man so he could well have been at a public school. And if he was, then the idea of shooting black men for money might not have seemed completely outrageous to him.'

It was an answer which might almost have pleased Sarah, he thought.

'Yes, but can you actually *see* him doing it?' asked Wilf.

'I don't know,' said Michael. 'It wouldn't surprise me. I'm sure he's got the stomach for it. Whether he's got — or had — the nerve as well, it's hard to say. Why so interested? You're not anticipating being attacked by bandits, are you?'

Wilf laughed. 'Shouldn't be surprised,' he said. He fell silent for a moment, then put on a serious look and lowered his voice.

'I gather you got involved last night, Mike,' he said. 'I'm sorry. God, I thought, that's terrible. A stranger. To inflict that on a stranger. But it's typical too. Typical. Terrible but typical. Well, look, Mike, forget it. That's all. Don't let it bother you. Pig in the middle's no place to be, I know it. I'm just sorry for the embarrassment to you and your charming wife. All right? Right!'

He patted Mike on the shoulder, forcing a halt, then turned away, took a couple of steps and turned back.

'You're a married man, Mike. You know how hard it can be. Tell me, what do you really think of her? Wendy, I mean.'

'I hardly know her,' said Michael cautiously.

'Me neither, I think sometimes. I could tell you things . . . but no, it's not right to involve other people.'

He paused invitingly, but Michael was too old a hand at uninvolvement to bite at such obviously hooked morsels.

'I'll say this, though,' resumed Wilf. 'I'm worried.

Really worried. This holiday was our last hope. You know, a fortnight in the sun. Rimini, Venice. Lots to do and see. A bit of old-fashioned therapy, but it's going to take more than that, I fancy. She's suicidal sometimes, you know. Oh yes. *Attempts*. Oh yes.'

He paused again nodding violently in emphasis. Michael stared at him aghast.

'Knocks you back, that does, eh?' said Wilf grimly.

'It does indeed,' said Michael, meaning it. He had not for one moment dreamt that Wilf and Wendy would be going on to Venice. In his mind there had been a division, now revealed as absurd, between those who lay on beaches and looked for Watney's Red Barrel and those who walked round art galleries and looked for beauty. He had, he realized, subconsciously assumed that he and Sarah alone would turn their backs on Rimini and head north next Tuesday. It would give Sarah great satisfaction if he revealed any of this to her. She was always energetic in identifying new areas of elitism in him.

On the other hand, he thought, I must pick my moment well for passing the news on to her. With a bit of luck there would be a momentary expression of horror on her face which could be put in the can and used in evidence.

'Well, that's my problem, of course,' said Wilf bravely, squaring his shoulders. 'You forget it, Mike. These things have a meaning, I suppose.'

This time he did walk away.

Michael watched him go with relief and went off in the opposite direction. It was an interesting old town, but by no means just a museum piece. The Buitoni factory belonged to the twentieth century and he was curiously pleased by its presence. But he found himself reluctant to search out 'The Resurrection'. It was as if he distrusted the adequacy of his responses and was fearful of testing them, just as more and more in recent years he had retreated from the world of violence and injustice with whose minions Sarah daily wrestled. What the hell, he thought. I've seen the film. And he paused to buy himself a straw hat against the sun. As he tried on his new purchase, he felt someone watching him and glanced round.

'Hello, Bob,' he said brightly.

Bob looked at his hat and nodded.

'It makes a change, a bit of peace and quiet,' said Michael.

'A change from what?' said Bob.

'From activity and noise,' said Michael pedantically.

'I suppose so. It's hot.'

This was the nearest to a social remark he had ever received from Bob.

'Yes, it is,' said Michael. 'It's very hot. Phew!'

He fanned himself with his straw hat in Chevalier fashion, making the most of this most perceptive comment.

'Phew!' he said again. Bob looked at him suspiciously. Despite the man's size and apparent stolidity, he was not a block, Michael reminded himself. He put his hat back on his head.

'Bob,' he said. 'Last night . . .'

'Look,' said Bob. 'I'm on holiday. What you do is your business as long as it doesn't affect me direct.'

'I see,' said Michael. 'Well, I'm sorry.'

'No, you're not,' said Bob. 'What you are is a bit of a clever bugger. Also a bit of a ram. Like I say, that's your business unless you're daft enough to make it mine. I thought last night you'd finally got that message.'

He clenched his right fist and wiped a line of sweat from his upper lip with the knuckles.

'Right. You're right,' said Michael.

'Good. Well, let's get on, shall we? Not much here.'

'Oh, I don't know. It has an atmosphere. It's the real thing, purely functional. Not just concrete money-making machines or even empty shells preserved for admiration. People live and work here.'

'Maybe so. People live and work where I come from. I could stop home and watch them if I wanted. No, I want to see something special for my cash. I hope next week's better than this.'

With sinking heart, Michael said casually, 'You're going on to Venice then?'

E

'Yes,' said Bob.

In silence they returned to the square where the car was parked. Michael examined the exchange as they walked. Bob's meaning was fairly clear. He believed that Michael had been trying it on with Molly till, warned off by Bob's demeanour, he had turned his attention to Wendy. By some Machiavellian device, Wilf had been lured out of his bedroom the previous night so that he, Michael, could pop in for a quick session. There was no obvious way of disabusing him of this idea.

Wilf and Dunkerley were already standing by the car in close confabulation. As Michael and Bob approached they broke apart and Wilf unlocked the car doors.

'All aboard!' he said. 'Quick as you can. Let's be off.'

Michael did not get in but asked, 'Where are we going? We'd better decide that first.'

'Well,' said Wilf, 'I've consulted our guide . . .'

'Our guide!' said Michael, raising his eyebrows. 'I *see*.'

'We ought to have a bit of a conference,' said Bob unexpectedly. 'We're all paying.'

'Of course. Democracy at work. Right-ho, Mike. What had you got in mind?'

'Well, as we've come this far we might as well go on a bit, and I thought it's not far to Arezzo . . .'

'Arezzo. What's that?'

'Charming spot,' said Dunkerley. 'Birthplace of Petrarch, Maecenas, Guido the musician, Bruni the historian, to name but a few. It was here that the Roman red pottery generally known as Samian ware originated. Also the birthplace of Vasari, author of *Lives of the Painters* whose house –'

'Isn't he great?' interrupted Wilf. 'Knows enough even for you, Mike. So, you're for moving on. You too, Bob?'

'Suits me,' said Bob.

'Me also. Well, that's what we thought. But not Arezzo. Who's heard of Arezzo? I mean, I can't go back and tell my kids I saw *Arezzo*, can I? But Syd tells me we can be in Florence in no time at all. Everyone's heard of Florence. So how about that?'

'But it'll make us very late getting back to the hotel,' protested Michael. What he meant was that Florence was too big, too beautiful. He didn't want to flit in and out of Florence in an evening. He wanted to save it up for some future occasion. But these were arguments he felt would carry little weight with Wilf.

'So we're on holiday! What's late?' demanded Wilf. 'Sydney here, he's got contacts in Florence, he tells me. Knows where to get us well fed and entertained. Are we game?'

'Suits me,' repeated Bob.

They climbed into the car.

A few miles further on they passed a group of young girls being shephereded along the side of the road by two white-habited nuns. It was a lyrical Fellini scene, chaste and sensuous at the same time. Wilf slowed down and blew his horn. The girls waved and the nuns smiled as Wilf made regal motions with his hand.

'Charming. Charming,' he said. 'Makes you feel like a fifteen-year-old, doesn't it?' adding with a bellow of laughter as he accelerated away, 'And with a bit of luck we might get one before the day's out!'

Sarah broke her usual rule and lunched in the dining-room that day. The weather was settling again and the beach was returning to normal, but she knew that a woman picnicking alone out there would quickly attract company. Also she felt responsible for Molly, although the younger woman did not accept her invitation to return to her old seat for lunch with any show of enthusiasm.

They had been sitting for several minutes drinking pineapple juice when Wendy joined them. Her outfit today was a sort of African tribal robe in boldly patterned cotton with a little turban to match. Sarah disapproved of the racial condescension implicit in the chic use of native costume, particularly from the underdeveloped countries, but had to admit the effect was striking.

'It's quiet without the children,' observed Wendy.

'I'm sorry?' said Sarah.

'The men. Thank God they're not here. It's the first

pleasant morning I've had since I came to this hole.'

Indeed, now Sarah observed her closely, she did look more animated than usual. The patina of make-up still lay thick on her cheeks, but her eyes had a lively sparkle instead of their customary dull glaze.

'I suppose it is nice to be able to please yourself,' said Sarah cautiously.

'It's nice not to be scared,' replied Wendy.

'Scared?'

'When that bastard's around, I'm scared.'

The waiter came, collected the empty fruit juice glasses and waited patiently while Wendy tasted hers, pulled a face and handed him the full glass.

'He hates me, you see. I make him feel guilty because I won't be unfaithful. I wouldn't mind, but what's the point? I did try it just once, but in the dark it might as well have been Wilf except that he took a bit longer. Mind you, if he knew he'd half kill me. Funny that, isn't it? As it is, he half kills me anyway. Do you enjoy sex? Personally I can't see anything to it. Not at all.'

The question was addressed to the air but Sarah took it to herself, partly because there seemed no chance whatsoever of Molly claiming it, but mainly because a frank open discussion was a challenge not to be refused.

'I think it's important,' she said. 'Our local Wollstonecraft society – it's a little group I helped found – held a seminar on it and it was fascinating to discover how many fears and misgivings were shared in common. Our conclusion was that it's as silly for us to feel that if you *don't* enjoy it, you're maladjusted as it was for the Victorians to believe that any woman who *did* enjoy it was wanton.'

'Wanting what?' asked Molly who had been following with close attention.

'I don't know anything about Victorians, but is it worth getting killed for, that's what I want to know,' said Wendy. She lit a cigarette, and Sarah, who detested smoking between courses almost as much as smoking in her bedroom, wrinkled her nose.

'No one's going to kill you for it,' she said reasonably.

'You can get killed for less than that,' asserted Wendy.

'Oh yes you can,' agreed Molly with an emphasis derived from Sarah could not guess what depth of experience.

'He said the other night he thought I was lesbian. Can you imagine being told that? What a foul thing to say. It made me feel ill just to hear him say it!'

'Well, there's no harm in being a lesbian,' Sarah felt constrained to say. 'I mean, the old prejudices really ought to be swept away, don't you think?'

Wendy stubbed her cigarette viciously in the plastic ashtray.

'Are you saying I'm a les?' she demanded.

'No, no. Not at all,' said Sarah hurriedly. 'All I'm saying is, if you *were*, there's no need to . . .'

'I know what I am. And I may not be an orgasm-a-minute wife, but I'm no lesbian. What do *you* know about *anything*!'

The main course arrived, slices of chicken cut very thin in an effort to disguise their toughness. At least, thought Sarah with a rare and intrusive flash of irony, it wasn't a meal calculated to stir up much of her guilt complex about the world's starving millions.

They ate in silence, Sarah collecting her thoughts, Wendy relapsing into a brown study more typical of her behaviour than her recent liveliness, and Molly (Sarah sensed) willing them both to recommence this exchange which she obviously found fascinating.

Nothing was said till the edible sections of the chicken were eaten and Wendy had lit another cigarette.

'Your husband seems all right,' she resumed in a friendly tone as though nothing of controversy had passed between them.

'Yes,' said Sarah.

'I know you never can tell. I mean, look at Wilf! But he seems nice. He's been very kind.'

'Has he?'

'Yes. I'm sorry he hurt himself.'

'When?' said Sarah, surprised.

'Last night. I wish mine would fall off a balcony. No,

I won't have any ice-cream. I'm trying to lose some weight.
Are you coming down to the beach?'

'I thought I'd stick by the pool today,' said Sarah.
'Just for a change.'

'You can't get a decent swim in that thing,' scoffed
Wendy.

'I'm not a very good swimmer.'

'That's all right. I'll look after you.'

Which was not what Sarah had meant at all, but it
seemed easier to go down to the beach than argue. Molly
joined them, bringing with her a thick historical romance
whose jacket seemed aimed at demonstrating the mutual
difficulties experienced by young men in pantaloons and
young women in farthingales.

After half an hour's relaxation in sunshine, now back
at full strength, Wendy suggested a swim. Molly refused.
She was completely immersed in her book and also bent
on grilling brown new areas of paleness revealed by an
almost indecently skimpy bikini which she was obviously
wearing for the first time. It was Bob's absence which had
caused the extra exposure, surmised Sarah, thinking
further that Michael would hardly care if she appeared in
two thimbles and an eye-patch.

The two women waded out till the water lapped their
thighs, then paused and stared out to sea.

'I sometimes think I'll finish myself off,' said Wendy.
'At least that way you know when it's coming. Do you
know what worries me most?'

'What?'

'That he'll bang me on the head and addle my brain.
He'd put me away as quick as a flash, you know. I
couldn't bear that, spending twenty years with a lot of
loonies.'

'For God's sake, Wendy! Why don't you leave him?'

'I don't believe in divorce,' she said seriously. 'Let's
swim.'

They pushed themselves forward and began to swim.
After twenty strokes Sarah rolled on her back and began
to float, but Wendy kept going and when Sarah looked
again, the sunflower hat was three hundred yards from

the beach and still moving away.

'Hey, signora!' someone called close by. She did not at first associate the call with herself, but when a splashing in the water behind her made her turn, she saw the smiling face of Aristide.

'Good weather now,' he said, white teeth flashing.

'Much better,' she said. 'How did you get on?'

She tried to stand on the bottom as she spoke to him and found the water was almost up to her chin. She hated to feel she was so nearly out of her depth and began to walk towards the shore, hoping her fear did not show.

'Did you find some lodgings?' she rephrased her question.

'I find,' he said, 'but it is not certain. I will ask Sydney. They cost very much. Perhaps too much. But it is season. It is time for rich tourists.'

He made a dismissive gesture and smiled again.

'Now I am tourist also,' he said. 'I enjoy.'

Taking a deep breath, he pushed himself half out of the water which was now breast high and duck-dived. She screamed as the water splashed into her face, and screamed again in real alarm as she felt her ankles gripped and forced apart. Then his long wiry body passed between her legs and he erupted behind her, shaking the water out of his hair and eyes and laughing once more.

'Now you do,' he said.

'Oh no. I couldn't.'

'Yes. It is easy.'

'No really. I don't like being under the water.'

'You don't like?'

'No. Really.'

'All right,' he said with a shrug. Have I offended him? she thought in alarm. Then he bent swiftly, pulled her legs from under her and sent her somersaulting backwards.

She came to the surface with her mouth full of water and her ears roaring. Her eyes stung and she could hardly see him before her, but she heard him laugh.

'Not like, eh? Not like.'

'You rotten sod!' she gasped, lunging towards him. He turned and ran, splashing with his arms in an effort to reduce the slow-motion effect of the water. She pursued him into the shallows till she was too out of breath to run any further and he stopped and turned. The water trickled down his dark brown body. He was very thin but with the leanness of a hound in training; his rib-cage was clearly visible and the thin chain of his bell charm lay along his breast-bone like the anchor cable of a wrecked ship. He wore a continental swimming costume, nothing much more than a leather pouch with a fringe of dark pubic hair sticking out of the top.

'I'll have to lie down,' gasped Sarah.

He nodded, went a few yards along the beach to retrieve his vest, slacks and sandals, then followed her to where Molly lay.

'You met Aristide last night,' said Sarah.

'Yes. Where's Wendy?'

'Jugoslavia I should think. I've swallowed half the sea. I'll have to have a drink. Aristide, it's your fault. Here, go and get me a Cola. Molly?'

'Yes, please.'

She gave the youth a five-thousand-lire note.

'And get whatever you want for yourself.'

'Merci, madame,' he said.

Molly watched him go with interest.

'Useful, isn't he?' she said. 'As well as pretty.'

'Pretty?'

'Nice-looking, if you like. Do you think Wendy really is a les?'

Sarah looked at her in astonishment. The shy quiet girl's role was to be seen and not heard.

'I don't know,' she said. 'I doubt it. Does it matter?'

'Of course it matters,' said Molly, with something approaching contempt. 'It matters to her and Wilf and to what we think of them.'

She was quite right, of course. All Sarah really knew about Wendy was a version of her marital problems, so some awareness of her sexual predilections was pretty essential if anything approaching understanding was to be reached. Being ignorant was not an essential ingredient of liberal tolerance.

'What do you think?' she asked.

'She's very strange,' said Molly. 'And she dresses funny.'

'So what?'

'Well, men do. Poofs, I mean.'

'It's a bit different,' protested Sarah.

'Is it? I don't know. That's why I'm asking. Bob hates anything like that. He got into bother once for hitting one of them.'

'Did he?' Sarah resisted the temptation to advance the theory that this probably indicated his own repressed homosexuality.

'Do you and Bob want a family?' she asked casually.

'Want? We've got three. A boy and twin girls,' said Molly, taking the ground from under her feet. Sarah viewed her stomach with envy. Now she looked, the evidence was there, but how well the girl had retained her figure.

'They're with their grandma. I needed a rest.'

'Mine too,' said Sarah.

'He beats her, you know. We've heard noises from their room.'

'Yes. We're on the other side,' said Sarah.

'I know,' said Molly significantly. 'Oh good. Here comes Jane.'

Sarah felt this was a bit cruel, even though Aristide certainly lacked the muscle to be Tarzan. The Cola was deliciously cold, like an anaesthetizing spray down the gullet. At home she would not allow the children to drink it, having read in a consumer magazine that it rotted your teeth, but here in the sun she craved it uncritically, like a pregnant woman.

Aristide lay on his back at her feet and sucked at his bottle like a baby.

'Do you work?' asked Molly.

'A job, you mean? No, not an actual job. But I run the house and kids, of course . . .'

'Oh, *that.*'

'And I'm *on* various things: local consumer group, neighbourhood crèche; then there's Oxfam, Help the Aged, several do-gooding things; as well as some political stuff, Labour Party, of course; and I'm doing an Open University course in sociology. So I'm kept fairly busy.'

'Yes, but you haven't actually got a job. I mean, is there anything you're *trained* for?'

Sarah found it difficult not to show how piqued she was by this dismissive response to her crowded and useful life.

'I did a commercial course, shorthand and typing, if that's what you mean.'

'Me too,' said Molly gloomily. 'Don't you sometimes get sick of being at home doing nothing all day? I could scream sometimes.'

Sarah forgot her pique instantly. Here was something she could understand and help with – the bored housewife/ second class citizen syndrome.

'You mustn't let it get to that stage,' she urged. 'Why not start working again?'

'I don't know. To tell the truth, Bob isn't very keen, not till the children are grown up a bit more. He thinks my place is at home. Anyway, I don't really fancy going back to an office, copy typing. I was just about as bored there. No, I've thought a lot about doing something else, you know, like becoming a teacher.'

Sarah nodded approvingly.

'That would be great. Why not? Have you gone into it at all?'

'I got some forms from a college near us that takes older students, but Bob didn't fancy the idea at all. He said that it was daft to go on a training course for three years when I could be earning good money somewhere else.'

'Which he doesn't want you to do anyway,' said Sarah grimly.

'I don't know what to do, really. He *is* my husband. I've been talking to Wilf about it. He's on an education committee, you know. He's been very helpful.'

'Ah,' said Sarah thinking that the kind of help Wilf was likely to offer to an educational novitiate could well be counter-productive.

'My husband's in education too,' she said. 'Why not talk to him?'

Michael wouldn't be very helpful, perhaps, but at least he wasn't so blatant with his erections.

'Thanks,' said Molly. 'But Wilf's at the top where the decisions are made. Did you get your change?'

'What?'

Molly nodded significantly towards the now apparently sleeping Aristide.

'I didn't see him give you your change.'

'No. He didn't. Not yet,' said Sarah.

'I'd watch him,' said Molly with a knowing nod.

Sarah felt irritated again. She could take the change of role from quiet mouse to feminist-guerrilla-in-the-making; indeed, she would do everything in her power to encourage the metamorphosis. But these woman-of-the-world hints were hard to stomach. She was still searching for some ironic reproof, superior without being patronizing when Molly disarmed her by saying, 'You won't say anything to your husband, will you?'

Sarah thought she might have misheard.

'*My* husband?'

'Yes. He's a bit *jokey*, isn't he? I wouldn't want him to say anything in front of Bob.'

A gush of sympathy washed away all Sarah's irritation. The girl automatically assumed her discretion. But men were lumped together as the enemy. *Jokey*; that was one way of putting it. As for Bob – Victorian paterfamilias; tun of lard settling ponderously down to his marital rites; guard dog lying across the exit from the prison which he and all the others like him had built for their women!

Surprised but not disturbed by the vehemence of her thoughts, she answered, 'No. I won't say anything.'

Aristide stirred, opened an eye, smiled up at her.

Sarah did not return his smile.

'Where's my change?' she said.

Wendy was drinking alone at the bar when Sarah came down for dinner.

'These prices are ridiculous,' she said. 'I can buy this stuff in Sainsbury's for what it costs here, and they're supposed to make it.'

Sarah examined her glass. It seemed to contain some kind of vermouth.

'They do give you a lot,' she said cautiously. 'You only get a thimbleful at home.'

'Do they? I never drink the stuff at home,' said Wendy.

'Oh. Why do you buy it?'

'I don't. I said I *could* buy it. But I don't.'

'You enjoyed your swim?' Wendy had still not returned when Sarah had decided to leave the beach and have a shower and an hour on the bed with *The Gulag Archipelago*.

'Yes.'

'You're very good. Did you do it competitively?'

'I was the best in my club and I swam for the county a few times.'

'Was Wilf interested?'

Wendy laughed like a seal barking.

'*Him*! He once followed me into my cubicle and tried to do me. Before a race! That was all he was interested in. There was talk of the Channel once.'

'The Channel!'

'Yes. I might have amounted to something. Aren't you drinking?'

'Well, thanks. I'll have the same as you.'

'Signora.'

It was Aristide, standing nervously a few feet behind her. After recovering her money from him, they had exchanged no more words and now the sight of him made her feel both irritated and guilty.

'Hello,' she said. Should she offer him a drink? Her hand went to the necklet he had given her. He smiled and nodded approvingly.

'Pretty,' he said.

That was surely worth a drink.

'Would you like a drink?' she asked and felt Wendy's disapproval beside her.

'No, thank you. The luggage, please. I would like to take it.'

'Of course!' she said. The poor boy. She had quite forgotten his bags. Perhaps he had wanted them earlier but had been afraid to ask.

She still had her key in her hand and she gave it to him.

'Help yourself,' she said.

'Thank you.'

Wendy watched him go over her glass.

'Anything valuable up there?'

'Not really. Why?'

'I'd say he'd done a bit of thieving in his time.'

'That's terrible. You've no right to say that,' Sarah protested weakly, remembering the beach that morning.

Wendy shrugged the subject away and lit a cigarette.

'I went through his insurances the other day,' she said. 'There's a lot. It's not for my benefit, of course. It's just that he values himself so highly. Has Michael got much?'

'I don't really know,' confessed Sarah.

'Of course, if he'd died on the plane coming over, he would have been worth another fifteen thousand. Don't you think separate flights make sense?'

'You're being a bit morbid, aren't you?' said Sarah. 'I dare say most people would rather go together if they have to go.'

'You're joking!'

'It can't be that bad, Wendy. If you want a divorce, that's one thing. But you wouldn't really wish him any physical harm, would you?'

'Listen,' said Wendy. 'Listen.'

She dipped her forefinger in her drink and carefully marked a spot on the polished bar. The barman yawned his contempt for package-deal tourists, but watched her with a glimmer of interest. Something about the tense curve of her athletic back (bared almost to the buttocks by a cutaway evening gown in purple and gold) and the frowning concentration of her face proclaimed this was real, this was earnest.

'See that,' she said. 'If that was a button, right? and pressing that button would set off a bomb in his head that would blow his eyes out through his nostrils, *watch*.'

Carefully she placed her thumb on the damp spot and pressed hard, maintaining the pressure till the flesh turned white around the scarlet thumbnail.

'Boom! Boom!' she said. 'That tramp's been gone a long time.'

'What?'

'He's been a long time collecting a suitcase. I would take a look if I were you.'

'Honestly, Wendy, you do go too far!'

'Do you want me to take a look?'

She shifted off her stool.

'No, thanks!' said Sarah hurriedly. 'I want to go upstairs anyway. I've left my handkerchief.'

She wondered to what extent Wendy's homicidal fantasies would ever be externalized. The woman needed treatment, that was evident. But what if the only real treatment were for Wilf to die, boom, boom?

At the door of her bedroom she paused, offended suddenly by a vision of Aristide rifling her belongings. Am I turning neurotic too? she asked herself, and went in.

There was no sign of Aristide but the suitcase and carrier lay on the bed. From the bathroom came the sound of running water.

'Aristide!' she called and pushed open the door.

He stood under the shower with a bar of Michael's herbal soap in his hand.

'Excuse,' he said with the inevitable smile.

Casually dropping the soap to the floor, he reached out for a bottle of her rather expensive medicated shampoo and poured half a pint over his head. A brief rub produced a huge aureole of foam. Despite herself, Sarah began to feel annoyed.

'What do you think you're doing?' she demanded stupidly.

He rinsed most of the bubbles out of his head and without bothering to switch the shower off he stepped out, seized a towel and began drying himself. The shampoo bottle fell on its side and began oozing greenily over the tiled floor.

'You've got no right!' exclaimed Sarah. 'You should have asked.'

'Asked? Why ask? I want to be clean. This is not

expensive to you, this water? I want clean. What's the matter? Am I too dirty to be clean here?'

He was beginning to look angry also.

'Of course not,' said Sarah. 'But . . . oh, look at my shampoo!'

She stooped to retrieve the bottle, but he was too quick. Picking it up, he held it over his head once more letting every drop of the green liquid trickle out.

'You stupid fool!' exclaimed Sarah, grabbing at the bottle, then, as she realized she was pressing against his damp body, jerking back.

As though symbolically, the necklet he had given her got tangled with his bell-charm and for a moment they were joined together like neighbours on a slave ship.

He reached out his hand to disentangle them, instinctively she jerked back again, the chains tightened. She attempted to undo the clasp but her fingers could not manage it and finally in an ambiguous rage, she took the necklet in both hands and snapped it.

At that moment there was a tap at the outer door and a voice called, 'Are you all right, Sarah?'

Unable to meet Aristide's gaze, Sarah turned on her heel, marched out of the bathroom, and opened the bedroom door to reveal Wendy's impassive face.

'Yes, I'm fine, thanks. Why shouldn't I be?' demanded Sarah, sliding out into the corridor.

'They're going in to dinner,' said Wendy. 'Has he gone?'

'Aristide? Yes. He's gone. Let's eat.'

As she pretended to lock the door behind her, she remembered the suitcase on the bed and wondered if Wendy had noticed. She didn't seem the observant type.

'Your dress looks a bit damp down the front,' said Wendy.

'Does it? Well, in this heat it'll soon dry.'

Molly was already at their table.

'The men aren't back,' said Sarah.

'You didn't expect them!' said Molly.

'I don't know. I hope Michael's not driving.'

'Not much chance of that with Wilf around,' said

Wendy. 'This minestrone's worse than the tinned stuff at home.'

Sarah pushed her soup away after a few mouthfuls. She was sitting facing the glass door between the dining-room and the foyer. Through it she glimpsed Aristide with his suitcase and carrier. He didn't glance her way but moved across the foyer towards the main exit. She thought of him under the shower. He had been so natural, so undisturbed, while she had behaved like a maiden aunt confronted by an exhibitionist. At least that was how she imagined she had felt. Or was her memory merely compensating for the suspicion that her surprise had inclined less towards outrage than desire? Which was worse? Outrage, of course. It was a betrayal of the basic dignity and equality of man and woman, whereas desire was merely a pseudo-betrayal of a social and artificial relationship. She pulled herself up. Only on rare occasions had she allowed herself to speculate on the possibility of being unfaithful to Michael. Sitting in a crowded dining-room with two other women at your table was not the right situation.

'I wonder what the men are doing now?' she said brightly.

'I shouldn't think about it,' said Wendy. 'It might put you off your dinner.'

Wilf kept on referring to the place as 'Sydney's club', as though hoping by the power of words alone to turn its shabby couches and scarlet wallpaper into old leather chairs and oak panelling. But Michael knew at a glance which end of *la dolce vita* they were at.

They had seen nothing of Florence. Half way there, they had run out of petrol, the fault Wilf claimed of an inaccurate gauge. It had taken a good hour to persuade one of the few cars also following the 'scenic route' to stop and give assistance. So, as 'Sydney's club' happened to be in the southern approaches to the city and as Wilf proclaimed himself completely starved, they had diverted straight here, leaving the central beauties for a post-prandial stroll.

The woman who ran the place was about fifty with a

face one side of which had been frozen by a stroke into a madonna-like serenity, while the other was a seething battleground for the warring emotions of greed and suspicion. She turned first one profile then the other as she negotiated fiercely with Dunkerley while the others watched from the car, and Michael had wondered if this was how it had felt to watch a medieval dumb-show.

A bottle of very cold Frascati was produced when Michael rejected the grappa he was offered and the icy wine refreshed him sufficiently to control his growing irritation and await events.

Dunkerley had left the room with the two-faced woman, allegedly to look at the menu.

'Well,' said Wilf, refilling his glass. 'This is nice. Homely. I know you like the real thing, Mike. Well, it doesn't come much realer than this.'

He looked with some complacency round the shabby but pleasantly proportioned room. Michael caught Bob's eye and they had their first moment of mutual sympathy.

Michael cleared his throat and asked, 'What's the plan, Wilf?'

'Well, a bite to eat. Syd says it's plain fare here but better than the tourist *ristorantes*. Can't move there, of course. Terrible. Then a look around if there's time. And home, back to the Leonardo and your lovely wives.'

Dunkerley returned, smiling.

'That's fixed,' he said cheerfully. 'A real Italian meal. Plus wine, very reasonable. Signora Beatrice is a fine cook. I think you will experience Italian provincial cooking at its best.'

'Don't we see what we're getting?' demanded Bob. 'Or what we're paying?'

Dunkerley looked at him with raised eyebrows.

'Forgive me,' he said. 'I'm sorry if it has not been made clear. This is not a restaurant. It is more of a – how shall I put it? – private – not club – but *meeting house*. Signora Beatrice entertains friends here and on occasion *their* friends. You are of course my guests and I shall take care of the meal.'

F

Michael liked *meeting house*. It had powerful religious overtones. Also the slightly affronted display of the mantle of *host* had been first class, but surely only a beginning?

'Of course, I regret that my relatively straitened circumstances cannot permit me to undertake the wine also, but I'm sure you will find Signora Beatrice's drink prices compare favourably with any bar.'

'That seems fair,' said Bob, a little set back. He poured

himself another glass of grappa to demonstrate that parsimony had not been the basis of his carping.

A girl came in, plump, rosy-cheeked, with long, hanging breasts surging beneath her blouse like ferrets in a sack. She smiled shyly at the men and began to arrange cutlery on the central table. They watched her in silence till she had finished and left.

'Now that's a bit of Italian provincial I'd like to experience,' said Wilf.

'As it happens,' said Dunkerley, 'we are quite fortunate tonight. Signora Beatrice has several young ladies in her employ. This is a large establishment and its upkeep requires a great deal of work. Two of them who are artistically inclined have been rehearsing an entertainment which they are willing to perform for us, should we be interested. It is, I believe, a form of exotic dance.'

He picked up the bottle of grappa, filled his own glass, then Wilf's and Bob's.

'On me,' he said. 'Michael, more wine for yourself, please. Here's to friendship. No heeltaps.'

They all drank.

'This dance,' said Bob. 'What do they do?'

'It is traditional. Etruscan in origin, I believe, though I have little knowledge of such things. A ritual propitiation of the forces of Nature is imaged. Another toast, gentlemen. The forces of Nature.'

They refilled and drank again.

'Yes, but what do they *do*?' insisted Bob.

'Do? Ah, not to put too fine a point on it,' answered Dunkerley, 'they screw each other. It is, of course, the old Beltane-Easter-Spring renewal thing. The return of fertility to the Waste Land.'

'With two *women*?' said Michael.

'There is nothing perverse intended,' said Dunkerley gravely. 'It is merely that the economic bases of domestic service make the employment of men a millionaire's privilege. The Elizabethan theatre's unisexuality was similarly constrained by social pressures.'

Michael laughed so much that he choked and it took a good half-pint of wine to ease his throat. Dunkerley looked offended, his naval beard jutting at a man-who-came-to-dinner angle, but before he could say anything further the door opened and the young girl entered bearing a tray with two tureens on it, and followed by the older woman with a couple of large flasks of Chianti.

'Behold,' said Dunkerley proudly, removing both tureen lids simultaneously to reveal a mountain of spaghetti and a pool of rather thin Bolognese sauce. He piled the food on plates which the girl distributed, dodging Wilf's amatory hand as she did so, while the Signora opened the wine. Michael tasted it and was comforted to find it excellent, but the food was another matter.

'Good?' enquired Dunkerley anxiously through a fringe of spaghetti.

'Oh yes,' said Michael, beginning to feel rather drunk. 'Tell the chef that Forte's of Watford Gap would not have been ashamed to serve it.'

'Ha ha,' laughed Dunkerley.

'What do they use?' asked Bob.

'Who?'

'These dancers. They must use something.'

'Well deduced. An instrument, alas. It does not assist the illusion. They would of course prefer the real thing.'

'Well,' said Wilf, 'if *that*'s all that's wanting to make them happy, perhaps we could help.'

Michael began to laugh again. It was the wine, of course. It was also this absurd charade of Wilf's to get them into a knocking-shop; it was the double-faced Signora and her revolting meal; and above all it was the diffident entry at that moment of two rather plain women, stark naked except for the monstrous rubber phallus one of them had strapped round her midriff. What Fellini could have done with this!

Close-up. A dove in flight. Below in early evening sunshine, the city of Florence. The dove wheels and banks, swoops down past Giotto's tower, Brunelleschi's dome, the Pitti Palace, the Ponte Vecchio, flutters on and on till finally it comes to roost on the roof of Signora Beatrice's 'club'.

Dissolve to interior; the two women grapple without enthusiasm. Wilf, face flushed with drink, his trousers round his ankles, tries to prise them apart. Dunkerley offers advice.

Split screen. The two sides of Beatrice's face look on, one with divine sadness, the other with diabolic cynicism.

A tangle of limbs and heads, how many it is hard to say. Like a single huge animal, the mass of bodies rolls over and over.

Quick cuts to and from the bodies, interspersed with shots of Michelangelo's David, Cellini's Perseus, Botticelli's Venus.

Close-up of a pair of male shoulders. A long-nailed hand digs into the base of the neck. Blood spurts. Everything freezes. A long cry fading bathetically into a nasal wheeze.

On the roof the dove deposits a blob of white and flutters away.

Dunkerley: SIGNORA BEATRICE IS HAPPY TO TAKE TRAVELLERS CHEQUES.

It was only nine o'clock when they left the house. Michael felt sober and rather sick. Only Wilf seemed to have gained in good spirits and vigour from the experience.

'The night is young!' he said. 'Time for more food. More drink. More everything!'

Michael shook his head. A quiet walk in the fresh air was all that he wanted. He no longer had any desire to see anything of Florence. Bob supported him and under Dunkerley's guidance Wilf drove them to a small park where he dropped them with assurances that he would return within an hour.

The two men walked in silence for a while. The park was quite crowded, mainly by family parties full of small children who by English standards should have been in bed hours ago.

'Not quite what I expected,' ventured Michael finally.

'You're your own boss,' said Bob.

'To an extent.'

'That's your problem,' sneered Bob.

'You mean *you* were in that house completely of your own free will!' demanded Michael. 'Will you tell your wife then, that you're so bloody possessive about?'

God! I'm still drunk, he thought in terror even as he spoke.

Bob turned on him and thrust his face close so that he smelled the grappa on his breath.

'Don't *you* go moral on *me*, lad,' he said. 'Not *you*.'

'OK. OK. I'm sorry. I'm sorry.'

'I was just *there*, that's all. Just *looking*. Right?'

'Whatever you say,' said Michael.

'Right then.'

Bob scrutinized him closely and Michael strained his features into a tough but sincere relief, like a Tracey/O'Brien priest facing a hoodlum.

'Right then,' repeated Bob, his expression relaxing. 'Right. Let's find a seat. I can still feel that drink.'

They sat down on a long bench between a nun and two angelic children.

'You got kids?' asked Bob.

'Two,' said Michael gloomily. 'They're quite nice but it can't last.'

'Why not?'

'They're in a neutral buffer state between Sarah and me. No intelligent person can spend an entire life in Switzerland. What about you?'

'I love my kids,' said Bob, who was sweating profusely and staring into the middle distance. Michael felt uneasily that his companion might be on the point of saying things he would regret later. He had no desire to be Bob's confidant.

'It's bloody warm,' he said.

'I want 'em brought up right. Discipline, that's the thing. A bit more home discipline would keep the crime figures down. But you can't have discipline without a sound home background. Regular meals. Someone in the house.'

'Ah, I see,' said Michael understandingly. 'What's the trouble? Bingo?'

'Don't talk daft! Does she look the kind of woman who'd get hooked on bingo? No, she wants to work.'

'Great,' said Michael. 'When the kids are old enough to look after themselves . . .'

'No!' said Bob emphatically. 'That's the mistake. Kids are never that old, some of 'em not even when the law says they are. Mine are just babies now. They'll need caring for over the next twenty years just about. I'm not bringing up tearaways and teenage tarts!'

'Of course not. Of course not,' said Michael soothingly. The two children attracted by the foreign language were peering up at the men with undisguised interest, and though the nun kept staring ahead with an expression of devotional half-wittedness straight out of *The Sound of Music*, Michael sensed that her ears were straining towards them.

'Doesn't Molly agree with you?' he asked in a low voice.

'I don't know. She keeps very quiet. I thought I'd shown her who was boss, but I don't know. It's funny. I wouldn't have believed it. They change, you know. You think when you marry 'em, you've got it all sorted; what you've got to offer, what they've got to do. It's all laid out. Me, I spelt it out, no misunderstanding. But they change. Who'd have thought she'd want to come on holiday without the kids? But here we are. I gave in. I thought it would help.' Bob was almost talking to himself.

'And has it?'

'Not so's you'd notice. She's worse, if anything. They've got you in a cleft stick, haven't they? You know what she said once? That if she couldn't have a life of her own with me, she'd have it without. Does that make sense? She was threatening to leave me! Can you believe it? Trouble is, the women always win. If she goes, who gets the kids? Not the man. Bloody stupid laws. So they'd be worse off than ever. She knows that. She doesn't say much, but she's deep, a lot deeper than she lets on. She'll be back there, thinking. That's probably why she didn't come today, so she could lie around all day thinking.'

'Well,' said Michael with ill-advised flippancy, 'it's better than lying around screwing.'

Bob turned and gripped his arm violently.

'Listen, you,' he said. 'You keep your nose out. And your nasty tongue. I've met your type. And I've chewed 'em up. And I've shit 'em out. Shit 'em! So watch it!'

He rose and strode away. The elder of the two children, a girl of about five, put her arms protectively round her smaller companion, but they did not budge. Only the nun's lips moved.

'Well, that was nice, Sister,' said Michael to her. 'I bet *you* don't get thumped after you've heard confession.'

The nun looked at him.

'*Non la capisco*,' she said.

'Huh!' said Michael, rising. 'Go and tell it to your beads.'

The journey back began nightmarishly. Wilf turned up half an hour late and very drunk. His awful cordiality now took on a manic quality and he wandered round the park, inserting himself noisily into family groups, offering the men a swig from his bottle ('grappa for pappa!'), leering at the women, and patting the children on the head ('hey, bambino!') with an audible crack. Something like a lynch-mob had begun to form by the time they got him back into the car. It was crazy to let him drive, but there was no other way of getting him in motion.

Dunkerley had been drinking too, but it showed only in a slight heaviness of gait and speech.

After half an hour, most of which Michael spent squatting on the floor in anticipation of the crash, they suddenly stopped and Wilf, who had been singing his way through *Hymns Ancient and Modern*, opened the door, fell out and was sick in mid-Amen.

It was very dark. They were in the middle of the country-side with no lights in sight.

'We *are* going in the right direction?' Michael asked Dunkerley.

'I believe so. Excuse me. I must piss.'

He clambered heavily out of the car and Michael followed him. The air was heavy and warm and full of the chirping of cicadas. He felt a sudden nostalgia for the cold breezes and subtler sounds of an English night.

They walked down the road a little, modestly getting into the penumbra of the headlights before halting.

Dunkerley swayed back and forward for a moment.

'Are you all right?'

'Yes, thank you. Your friend is a hard man to keep up with.'

'You seem to have managed. At least you're not puking.'

'True. Tell me, Michael, would you say that Wilf is in any degree unbalanced?'

'What?'

'Is he, would you say, deranged?'

'I don't know. He's certainly very extrovert, but I wouldn't have said deranged. I mean, he's on holiday. We all let ourselves go on holiday. Why do you ask?'

'Mrs Trueman,' said Dunkerley. 'I have not so far in our brief acquaintance had much to do with Mrs Trueman. She is the plumpish lady who sits apart and makes the occasional oracular utterance?'

'That's her,' said Michael.

'Are relations between them at all strained?'

'I hardly know them,' said Michael cautiously. 'I said, why do you ask?'

Dunkerley let go a final burst and buttoned himself up.

'Earlier,' he said, dropping his voice. 'Earlier when Wilf and I were drinking together, he quizzed me at some length about my service record. Morbid curiosity, I thought. A not uncommon reaction. But I was wrong.'

'Why?' asked Michael. 'What did he want?'

'He wanted to know,' said Dunkerley, 'how much I

would charge for killing his wife.'

They got back to the Leonardo at 2 a.m. Bob had told Wilf he was going to take over the driving and Wilf, first belligerent, then petulant, had hurled the keys into the darkness. It took them twenty minutes to find them, by which time he had turned maudlin and was apologizing incessantly and tearfully. Half an hour later he had recovered sufficiently to sample his San Marino brandy, and as they walked through the hotel door, he was under full steam again.

The juke-box was dark, one of the waiters was doing some desultory cleaning up and only two people remained drinking in the lounge: Sarah and Molly.

'This is devotion! This is true love!' declared Wilf, attempting a simultaneous embrace. 'But who's absent, eh? Who's absent?'

'Wendy's just gone up,' said Sarah defensively. 'She went for a little walk along the beach to liven herself up, but she was really tired.'

'Tired, was she?' sneered Wilf. 'Slaving over a hot stove all day, perhaps? Or reading an improving book? Tired! You see what I have to suffer, gents. Some men have wives who cossett and comfort 'em, but not me. She'd sit up long enough for my funeral, oh yes. She'd sit up if they said they were bringing me back in a hearse, but just to make sure, that's all. But I'll surprise her, I'll outwit her, never you fear. There ain't no flies on old Wilf. No indeed.'

He set off up the stairs.

'Don't you think you should see to him?' asked Sarah.

'He'll be all right,' said Michael.

'I wasn't thinking of *him*,' snapped Sarah.

There was a crash followed by a curse and a snatch of 'Now The Day Is Over'.

'I'll sort him,' said Bob. 'Come on, love.'

He set off, but Molly did not move.

'Come on!' he ordered, pausing and turning.

'I'll just finish my drink,' she said.

He glowered at her for a moment, then marched

angrily from the lounge.

Michael, whom the stresses of the journey had sobered up completely, examined the situation with care. It was obviously confrontation time. He felt ill-prepared both physically and morally for confrontation. He put on his talking-to-the-principal smile.

'Have you had a nice day?' he asked.

'Splendid,' said Sarah.

'Good. That's good. Well, if you don't mind, I'll push on upstairs. All this driving's worn me out.'

'Where did you go?' demanded Sarah.

'Oh, hither and thither. Florence eventually.'

'Florence! You never said you were going to Florence!' protested Sarah. 'You *know* I've always wanted to go to Florence.'

'I'm sorry. It was unpremeditated. I had no idea. I wasn't in control.'

'Florence! What did you see? Did you go to the Uffizi and the Vecchio Palace? I did an extra-mural course on Florence once, Molly, and I have been dying to go ever since. Did you see where Giuliano was stabbed and Savonarola burned? Have you got a guide-book? May I see it?'

Florence, though the only Italian city with which Sarah had even a vicarious acquaintance, had not figured large in their pre-holiday discussions. Indeed, all that Michael remembered of this particular extra-mural course (one of a long series ranging from Chinese poetry to The Sociology of the Urban Guerrilla) was that Sarah had had a row with the lecturer about Cosimo Medici's exploitation of the labour force. Normally he would have mocked these allegations of deprivation unmercifully, but his position was weak.

'We didn't see a great deal,' he said. 'It was quite late when we got there. We'd stopped in Sansepolcro on the way. Where Piero della Francesca's "Resurrection" is.'

'Oh. What's that?'

'Aldous Huxley said it was the greatest painting in the world.'

'Did he?' Michael saw Sarah tucking the information

carefully away. But she was not going to be diverted.

'But what about Florence? Tell me about Florence. You must have seen *something*!'

'Excuse me,' said Dunkerley.

Michael thought he was attempting a rescue and felt grateful, but the man continued, 'I wonder if you happen to know the whereabouts of my young travelling companion. I thought to have met him here on our return, but we are a trifle late.'

'I'm sorry,' said Sarah. 'He found lodgings, he told me that, but he thought they might be too expensive. Then he collected his luggage this evening and left.'

'His luggage?'

'The bag and the case, both.'

'Oh dear. This is most unfortunate. He left no message?'

'None. Except that he wanted to consult you before accepting the terms.'

'Most unfortunate. These young men, they have no thought for others. No thought.'

Dunkerley turned and shuffled off across the tiled floor towards the beach exit. To Michael's surprise, Sarah made no effort to prevent him. He must have done something very nasty to dry up her almost inexhaustible springs of social sympathy. Michael went after him and overtook him by the swimming pool.

'Where will you sleep?' he asked.

'How kind you are. Don't worry, my dear chap. I shall be very snug out here on one of these reclining sun chairs. The hotel staff will all be a-bed by now. I shall be undisturbed. Most kind of you to ask.'

'You're sure?'

'Of course. Now go back to your charming wife. Good night, dear boy.'

Michael turned away, but Dunkerley laid a hand on his arm.

'Just one word, Michael. What I said to you earlier about Wilf. I was a little drunk I fear. A joke, no more. In bad taste, but only a joke. You paid no heed I'm sure.'

'Of course not,' said Michael.

'Good. Then good night again. Splendid day. Splendid.'

Yes, it had been for you, thought Michael. Food, drink, a woman – or at least a share – and a nice percentage from Signora Beatrice. Splendid indeed. But the night was too warm and fragrant, the sound of the nearby sea too seductive for resentment. He breathed deep, his recent nostalgia for the night air of England now forgotten. This richer element contained possibilities almost un-thought-of on that chilly island.

As he passed through the lounge, he did not permit a resumption of the Florence catechism but said without pausing, ' 'Night, Molly; 'night, darling. Rather tired. I'll have a shower and get my head down.'

He hoped to be showered and in bed before Sarah arrived, but he was still towelling himself when the door opened.

'Have you been using my herbal soap?' he asked.

'No. You know I don't like it. It smells of sage and onions.'

'Someone has. It must be you. Who else would take a shower in our room?'

'You're imagining things,' she said. 'Tell me about Florence. What *did* you see?'

He hung up the towel and walked across the room to the bed.

'Not much,' he said pulling back the coverlet. 'The Ponte Vecchio, Santa Croce, Giotto's Lily Tower, the usual things. What the hell's this?'

'Michael, what *have* you been doing?'

Lying under the top sheet and partly concealed by the pillow as if it had fallen off unnoticed was a thin silver chain. He picked it up. A small silver bell tinkled as it swung in his hand.

He turned to Sarah.

'You've been with someone!' she said.

'What?' The sentiment was so much his own that he was bewildered for a moment.

'You should be careful,' she said, her voice strained in the attempt to affect indifference. 'You'll get blood poisoning.'

He turned to the wardrobe mirror and, twisting his head to get a view of his back, he saw a double line of scratches running from his neck along his shoulder-blade.

Oh shit! he thought looking at Sarah again. She was quite pale. He held the chain before him and shook it gently.

'Send not to know for whom the bell tolls,' he said.

Through the wall they heard Wendy start to weep.

I

'Ladies. Gentlemen. We are now approaching the Rubicon.'

Michael closed his eyes and, as anyone in his position would do, started thinking about Visconti.

'This is the river which in the days of Ancient Rome marked the boundary between Italy and Cisalpine Gaul.'

Sarah thought about Aristide. His gesture of leaving the bell-necklace in her bed was capable of many interpretations, ranging from passionate desire through pity to malice. She had built fantasies on each gradation. She had come late to a fantasy-life and was amazed at the exciting vistas it had opened up for her. The first step had been to make no attempt to disabuse Michael of his belief that Aristide had made love to her. She had never deceived him before in anything and at first had not recognized this as a deceit. But she knew it now and knew also that deceit is of the mind as well as the body. In a way the mental deceit was worse – and more exciting. The physical was usually kept secret and private while the mental was performed in public.

'When Caesar crossed this boundary with his army in 49 BC he was in effect declaring war on the Republic of Rome.'

The essence of Visconti's *Death in Venice* was of course the decay of creativity. What a perfect image the city was, with its incredible beauties reaching into the air while its very foundations were being gnawed and sucked at by a dark force, half sea and half sewer. So ambivalent also was the attraction Aschenbach felt for the beautiful boy. So ambivalent also were all relationships, thought Michael. He wished heartily he could undo what had happened two nights ago. To be discovered having fucked a common whore hurt his pride.

'Watch carefully. It is a very narrow river. You can pass it without noticing.'

The scene could not be edited out. But it could perhaps be played again with better direction.

'Ladies and gentlemen. We have crossed the Rubicon,' said Dunkerley.

'Excuse me,' said Sarah. 'I want to have a word with Aristide.'

She rose and walked up the aisle of the bus. Dunkerley in the front seat immediately behind the driver toyed with his microphone like a new mayor with his chain of office. His cultivation of the hotel courier had borne fruit. She had not relished the idea of a hot day in a coach just to dump a party of tourists into a Venetian hotel. Also one of her children was ill and Dunkerley's offer to take charge of the trip in return for a ride to Venice plus her meals on route had tempted her. When he produced evidence of his experience in the form of a pre-audition of his journey commentary she had given in.

Aristide had been part of the deal.

He sat alone beside the door and did not look up as Sarah joined him.

'Hello,' she said. 'How are you?'

'I am tired,' he said, closing his eyes. 'I will sleep.'

He pouted his lips sulkily and performed such a dreadful mime of repose that Sarah might have been amused had she been frivolous enough to find humour in serious situations.

'I'd like to talk to you,' she insisted.

'Why? You are kind one day. Then you change. Yesterday you do not look at me. Why?'

It was true. After a sleepless night she had spent an uncertain day in which she wanted to do nothing but separate her real from her imagined wounds and lick them. Nothing else had moved her, not Wendy's black eye, nor Molly's attempts to resume their discussion of her break for freedom, nor even the chaotic police activity following the discovery of a body under a boat only a quarter of a mile along the beach.

'I'm sorry,' she said. 'I was preoccupied. Worried. I had no time to talk to anyone.'

'Worried? What is there to worry? This is your holiday. Nothing to worry.'

He was sulking still, but taking notice now, enjoying his sulk. Normally Sarah had little sympathy with such emotional games. Life was too short and too earnest for anything but absolute honesty, or at least as much as the social traffic would bear. But now she found herself amused by the youth's desire to be coaxed back to good humour. The feeling was, she assured herself, maternal, though such behaviour in her own children had never won much sympathy.

She produced the bell-necklace.

'You left this,' she said.

'Yes. The other break. I am sorry. It is cheap, I have little money. But this is better, I think. When you hear it, you think of me. Listen.'

He took the bell and shook it. Down the bus, Michael's head lifted momentarily.

'See,' said Aristide cheerfully. 'Your husband, he think of me.'

'Yes,' said Sarah. 'I dare say he does.'

Something in her tone must have reached the young man despite the poorness of his English, for he looked at her now with a gaze most shrewd and knowing and said, 'Your husband is jealous? Not so? Why? Ah!'

He tinkled the bell once more.

'In the bed! He finds this in the bed!'

'Yes,' said Sarah. She had not been going to say anything of this, of course, but now it was said she saw no reason to deny it.

'He is foolish!' proclaimed Aristide, white teeth flashing in a broad grin.

'Oh, is he?' said Sarah. 'Thank you.'

Again he got the subtlety behind the simple words.

'No, please. Not because of you. Beautiful Sarah, good to be in bed with! Foolish because of this!'

The bell again. Sarah had the feeling that every ear in

the bus was tuned in on their conversation.

Absurdly she felt impelled to defend Michael.

'No,' she said. 'Not just that. You had a shower too. You used his soap.'

'Ah,' he said thoughtfully. 'Ah.'

'What will you do in Venice?' asked Sarah, feeling it was time now for a change of subject.

'I shall see everything. Taste everything. Touch everything.'

He made an expansive gesture in which one of his hands brushed her breast. It was so accidental he did not even apologize.

'Have you been before?'

'Never. Sydney, he has been. Everywhere he has been.'

'That is not precisely true, dear lady, but making allowances for Gallic hyperbole, it will do.'

Dunkerley, who had been unashamedly eavesdropping, leaned over and tapped her on the knee with his microphone, a gesture lifted from an eighteenth-century drawing-room with fans fluttering like pinions in some ornithoid mating display.

Was Dunkerley queer? she wondered. Not that it mattered, of course. Freedom of sexual fulfilment was one of the keystones of any truly advanced society. So long as it did not hurt others. She looked at Aristide anxiously. He was a handsome boy. Could this be why Dunkerley had taken him under his wing? Perhaps he really needed the help of a woman to keep him on the straight and narrow. But her own liberal conscience told her that there was no straight and narrow; all ways were broad and winding. In any case the therapeutic sexual act was a male chauvinist concept, designed to facilitate masculine abuse of the female body. It was the age of the democratic orgasm. Michael's might be more frequent than her own, but it certainly wasn't more equal.

But I'm not thinking about Michael, she scolded herself. I'm thinking about Aristide. Do I really want him?

The answer unfortunately was no. There was not a great deal of sensuality in Sarah's make-up, and though she sometimes regretted it, she scorned to pretend to it.

G

What Aristide represented was a non-existent act of infidelity of which she had been found guilty and condemned to pay God knows what penalty. In other words she was in credit for one bout of illicit intercourse. As her stern but provident mother had said as she stood over her daughter each week while she reluctantly put half of her pocket money in a piggy bank, 'It's a comfort to have something behind you.'

The direction signs drifted past like the sibyl's leaves bearing incomplete and half understood messages. Ravenna, Ferrara, Este, Padova, places which surely could only be reached by time-machines or yellow-brick roads? And at the end of it all, Venice, La Serenissima, floating on the lagoon like an Arabian mirage. Michael watched for the miracle to be revealed, watched patiently along the dull miles of autostrada, watched suspiciously along the pylon-lined causeway across what looked like a section of the Essex marshes, and watched incredulously as the coach slowed down to enter a hell called the Piazzale Roma. Road traffic can go no further in Venice, proclaimed Dunkerley, and as if giving vent to the frustration of beasts held up short of their natural prey, lorries, coaches and cars snarled and roared and milled round in herds from which blue exhaust fumes rose like prairie dust. Over all towered the first Venetian building of any note which Michael had seen in the bricks and mortar, or rather concrete – a multi-storey car park.

'Just like home,' observed Wilf. 'Here, I can see your room, Mike.'

He pointed up at the top floor of the car park. Michael smiled wanly and joined the shuffle out of the coach. Sarah had sat with Aristide for about half an hour, returned to his side briefly, then gone down the aisle to join Molly who was sitting by herself, ostensibly so that both she and Bob could enjoy a window seat, but clearly because of a row.

He paused to let Wendy ease herself into the aisle ahead of him.

'All right?' he asked.

She turned her discoloured eye towards him.

'He wants me dead, you know,' she said. 'That's what it'll come to.'

'Oh, I doubt it,' said Michael reassuringly, thinking that her make-up looked as if it had been applied to accentuate rather than disguise the discoloration.

'Remember me,' she said.

Outside in the carbon-monoxide-rich heat, Dunkerley was organizing things with a smoothness derived, Michael assumed, from his African experiences. Presumably a live mercenary was an efficient mercenary, though in that case why Dunkerley should be bumming his way round Europe was a mystery. Perhaps a failure of nerve. Michael tried to imagine being shot at.

Medium shot. A line of trees, foliage trailing to the ground. The leaves shake gently, reflecting sunlight from their polished surfaces.

Close-up. His face, sweat-beaded, eyes flickering from side to side as he tries to gauge what made the leaves move. Then shots. A fusillade. Eyes widen, no longer flickering.

Medium shot. His body erupting blood from numberless holes slides to the ground where it lies still, twitching in posthumous spasms as the bullets continue to pour into it. Now we hear his shriek . . .

'If you would take your own cases, ladies and gentlemen, it will result in expedition.'

It did, and ten minutes later they were crammed in a *vaporetto* thrashing its way along the Grand Canal, and suddenly despite the crush of people, the engine shuddering beneath his feet, the proximity of the Piazzale Roma, the sound of Wilf's voice raised in raucous mimicry of an Italian tenor, the miracle happened. Venice, La Serenissima, shimmered on all sides like an Arabian mirage.

Their hotel, teetering like a drunk on the thin line between third and fourth class, offered the consolation of being fairly close to the Piazza San Marco and that first journey took them the whole length of the Grand Canal. Michael's mind was working like a full production team, darting in and out of side canals and palazzi, composing, framing, mixing, overlaying, pulling back from detailed close-ups to panoramic sweeps, knowing that there was too much here, that he was just providing treadage for the cutting-room floor but unable to resist.

'Aren't you going to take any pictures?' asked Sarah, who had returned to his side.

He laughed aloud but said nothing. They had passed beneath the wooden Academy bridge and ahead the waters broadened out as the Grand Canal ran once more into the lagoon. On the right the tower and dome of the island church of San Giorgio Maggiore took some eyes, but to the left there came into view that most breathtaking of sights, the powerful, dramatic and unforgettable image which all great cities must possess if they possess any real claim to greatness – the soaring campanile, the oriental façade of the Doge's Palace, between them the granite columns of St Mark and St Theodore flanking the entrance to the Piazzetta San Marco, and, beyond, the domes of the great basilica itself.

'Isn't it splendid!' cried Molly.

Bob controlled his emotions well and returned only a grunt, but Wendy, lighting a cigarette, paused to say in her flat, hopeless voice, 'Yes, it's very pretty.'

For a moment Michael felt like offering his wife-disposing services free of charge to Wilf, but the man's own voice came next, saying, 'Of course, it's an open sewer all this water. Just take a sniff. Filthy sods, aren't they? Wouldn't do back home, I tell you. Local health snoops come round my shop, they think meat shouldn't bloody well bleed!'

He saw a sudden still from Chabrol's *Le Boucher* – the shop, the meat, the broad-bladed knife, but the psychotic butcher had Wilf's face.

Their hotel bedroom was small and stuffy and over-looked a side-alley so narrow that it was doubtful if the sun ever penetrated here. The window opposite was almost touchable by an outstretched hand. Only the presence of a dimly perceived figure behind the dusty glass prevented Michael from trying the experiment as he leaned out in search of air. Below, at the corner of the alley where it joined the wider *calle* on which the hotel was situated, stood two figures. One was Aristide, the other Wilf. The latter pressed something into the former's hand. Both seemed to be talking at once. They parted.

A tip? wondered Michael. Aristide and Dunkerley were now presumably going to slip into the city's sub-life with which the fat man was doubtless as familiar as that of Florence. He felt a quick stirring of the flesh as he recalled the whore's long reddened nails raking his skin at the climax.

'Aren't you unpacking?' demanded Sarah.

'Yes. In a moment. There's not much room.'

He watched her carefully unfold her dresses and hang them in the huge wardrobe which occupied rather more space than the bed. How did they get such pieces of furniture here in the first place? he wondered. And why didn't he want to think about Sarah? It was the holiday, of course. It was so limiting. You couldn't have a final, irreversible separation when you were both on one passport. Curious that her feminism had never spewed out protests at that. No, holidays did not cater for the serious things of life, like divorce, disease, and death. With a bit of luck they might see a funeral gondola while they were here. Why should Wilf tip Aristide?

The room had a washbasin but no shower or lavatory, and though the brochure had implied that the hotel was so full of bathrooms that it was making a major contribution to Venice's slow decline into the lagoon, Michael had only noticed one, fortunately right next door to their room. He now approached the other wall and listened.

'What are you doing?' asked Sarah.

'I'm just checking whether we're likely to get a good night's sleep,' said Michael.

'You're totally selfish, aren't you, Michael?'

He considered the question, but felt no need to offer an answer. Which, he supposed, was an answer in itself. Though of course it could be argued that the totally selfish man could not by definition be aware of his total selfishness.

'Let's see what lunch is like,' he said. 'I'll unpack my stuff later.'

'Oh, go on. I'll do it, otherwise it'll be creased to pieces. I'm not very hungry.'

'I just want something light,' said Michael.

As he descended the stairs he thought how easy it was to preserve an armed truce if circumstances required it. Like the unofficial Christmas peace in 1914, it could continue indefinitely, barring accidents or a direct command for hostilities to be resumed. Yesterday had been rather tense, but the difficulty of being alone, the holiday atmosphere, the sense of routine, had all contributed to a postponement of the final scene which they were both rehearsing in their minds. Sarah had been a bit distant but she had not been able to disguise her interest when ripples from the police activity three hotels away had reached them. She had refused to join him in a stroll along the beach to the scene of the crime, but had listened closely (though pretending to read) to his lively account (subtly exaggerated in a Billy Wilder way) of the clash between the *Guardie di Pubblica Sicurezza* and the *Carabinieri* about investigatory rights. Something to do with high-tide mark, he guessed satirically.

She would never forgive him, of course, but she might forget. He toyed with the idea of asking for all his other offences to be taken into consideration. The thought that she might believe that his extra-marital adventures were confined to professional tarts, purchased in drink, really offended him, but it was difficult to contrive a situation in which a general confession would not sound like either remorse or malice. Or, worst of all, imagination.

Anyway why shouldn't she forgive him? She was after all a liberated woman with no antediluvian moral taboos. Let her practise what she preached.

'Oh Jesus!' he said and leaned against the wall. It was incredible, but he kept forgetting he was a cuckold. He too had been sinned against, he too had to decide whether to forgive or merely forget. And she did not even have the excuses of drink, Dunkerley and masculine frailty. The thought of her and that skinny French boy made him sick.

He should have struck her. He couldn't imagine why he hadn't.

'Are you all right?'

It was Molly managing to look concerned and antipathetic at the same time.

'Yes. The bus journey and the heat. I'll be fine.'

'Can I give you a hand?'

'No.'

He took a step, felt weak and gratefully grasped at Molly's offered arm.

'Thanks,' he said. Her bare skin was surprisingly cool. He let his hand slide up to her shoulder. It was slight and bony, like a boy's.

'You!'

A hand gripped his shirt from behind and pulled him backwards.

'Bob!' protested Molly.

'I've told you before,' said Bob.

'He's sick.'

'That's obvious. Listen, I won't tell you again. You practise somewhere else. All right?'

Michael nodded.

'You stupid great ape!' exploded Molly, and turning on her heel she walked away.

'Molly!' said her husband incredulously. He went lumbering after her and Michael after a moment resumed his search for the dining-room. He felt very well now and very peckish and after lunch all Venice awaited him.

Sarah appeared as he was finishing his coffee and contented herself with a peach. She ate a lot of peaches in Italy, perhaps because she could be certain they did not come from South Africa or Spain. Thank God Portugal was for the moment all right.

'Shall we explore?' he asked.

'No. It's too hot for me. I just want to rest for an hour. You go on, though.'

He shrugged, not understanding how anyone could rest with all this outside the door.

'All right,' he said.

'Don't overdo it,' she called after him. He paused and looked back at her. Was she laughing to herself?

Outside he followed the drift of tourists till he reached St Mark's Square. For a long time he just stood and let the pictures scald his mind. The square was like a giraffe – absurd, impossible, and beautiful beyond computation, as if Michaelangelo, Christopher Wren, Walt Disney and God had sat in committee to build it.

He turned slowly in a full circle, then once more, and once more. The square was crowded, but the other people were to him mere faceless extras, paid to wander aimlessly round and round.

Then he stopped with his back to St Mark's. To his right, strolling along in the cool shadow of the arcade of the Procuratie Vecchie, he glimpsed a figure in a bright red shirt. The square was full of garish colours; this was a place for them; there was no sense here of historical incongruity. But this single red shirt glimpsed distantly and intermittently as its wearer moved along behind the arcade's columns caught and held his eye. He was instantly and completely convinced it was the boy from Rimini. The irrationality of this was so great that he felt it simultaneously, but with no diminution of conviction. And when he set out in pursuit, it was not to test a theory but to confront a foe. Forcing a way through the crowds was difficult. Gaps opened, then closed as he pressed towards them. Family groups in solid phalanx made him divert. A young Italian taking photographs shouted at him as he bumped into his tripod, and two Japanese girls with handfuls of bird-food set a screen of whirring pigeon wings between him and his prey. The extras were being directed by Hitchcock, he told himself. Then with a masterly timing, he was permitted through, ahead was an almost empty expanse of square and, disappearing through one of the archways of the Napoleonic wing, was the red-shirted boy.

Michael broke into a trot, but the boy was not in sight when he reached the welcome shadow of the arcade. He hesitated a moment. The entrance to the Correr Museum was here. Could the boy have gone in there or would he have continued straight ahead through the rather gloomy passage which must lead to the streets beyond the piazza? He made a quick decision and went forward, turning left, then right. The crowds were here again and he began to feel his task was hopeless. He passed a big ugly church, the first distasteful building he had seen in Venice (he didn't count the Piazzale Roma as part of the city) and then found himself in a relatively broad street full of antique shops and banks. Ahead just turning right was the red shirt. Or at least *a* red shirt. He was no longer so certain of himself, but the hunt was up and a man must follow. Another long street with not a red shirt in sight. He hurried along, glancing into shops and bars, till the street broadened out into a campo which contained the inevitable church and another building which felt familiar. When he approached nearer he realized what it was, the Teatro La Fenice where the marvellous opening scenes of Visconti's *Senso* took place. This discovery almost diverted him from the chase, but when he gave what was intended as a final cursory glance around the campo the red-shirted boy was standing in the shadow of the church and looking directly towards Michael.

'Hey you!' shouted Michael.

The boy seemed to smile, turned, and slipped out of sight through the church door. Michael had taken a couple of paces after him when he felt his arm seized.

'Don't look now,' said a voice.

'What!'

He twisted round, dragging himself free from the grip at the same time.

It was Dunkerley, smiling knowingly.

'I was going to say, don't look now, but your religion's showing.'

'What the hell are you talking about? And what are you doing here?'

'Like yourself, I suppose. Gazing on beauty. I saw you staring at the . . . church.'

'Did you see a boy over there? Eighteen, nineteen perhaps. In a red shirt.'

'There was a young man, I believe,' said Dunkerley. 'The city is full of youth.'

'Had you seen him before? The night I met you at the bus stop in Rimini, do you recall him on a motor-scooter?'

Dunkerley considered.

'There were some youngsters on scooters, I recall. But show me an Italian city where they do not proliferate! Except here in Venice, of course.'

He laughed, then shook his head.

'No, I cannot bring to mind a particular face. You think you know this boy?'

'I think it's the same one.'

'Well, it's easy to check. My translation talents are at your disposal. He went into the church, you say?'

'Yes.'

'Come on then.'

They entered the church. It was empty. Michael realized he had not expected anything else.

'Gone, it seems,' said Dunkerley. 'Note the fine chancel, though. A design of Sansovino's, I believe.'

'Is there another way out?' demanded Michael.

'My dear fellow! They have more escape hatches than a submarine, these places. Being religious never stopped Italians trying to kill each other in church!'

They went out again into the sun-filled campo.

'Let's have a drink,' suggested Dunkerley. 'I know a place, quite close. The true Venetian ambience, none of your tourist traps.'

'Is the true Venetian ambience anything like the true Florentine ambience?' enquired Michael, able now that the scent had gone cold to give his full attention to the fat man.

'Not at all,' assured Dunkerley. 'Though that could be arranged.'

'No, thanks,' said Michael. 'A glass of beer will do me.'

Dunkerley did his Oliver Hardy act with a Punt e Mes while Michael took a long draught of his ice-cold German beer and wondered what the purpose of this socialization was.

'This young man from Rimini,' said Dunkerley. 'A friend?'

'Not really.'

'Just someone you made contact with?'

'You could put it like that.'

'Ah,' said Dunkerley. 'I see.'

He sipped his drink and closed his eyes to savour the taste.

'I think I may be able to assist you,' he said. 'Shall we have another drink?'

Michael was puzzled. Assistance from a man like Dunkerley would certainly cost high. But what on earth could he offer?

'I don't think you understand,' he began as Dunkerley summoned a waiter with a confident snap of the fingers.

'I understand everything.'

Suddenly the bearded man shook his head, just a single movement as though to dislodge an insect, but as he repeated the order to the waiter, Michael glanced over his shoulder. It was his day for brief glimpses, it seemed. But he was ninety per cent sure that the slim figure just moving from sight about twenty yards down the *calle* was Aristide.

'Was that your side-kick?' he asked.

'My . . .? Aristide, you mean? It may have been.'

'Why did you warn him off? Am I supposed to be about to punch him on the nose?'

This seemed to amuse Dunkerley, then he composed his features in a naval seriousness such as might have become a captain just instructed to sink the *Bismarck*.

'You fear he may have made approaches to Mrs Masson?'

'I fear nothing about him or about you, Mr Dunkerley,' said Michael coldly.

'Of course not. Why should you? Tell me, Michael, do you have children?'

'Yes. Two. Why?'

'Interesting, that. They are being looked after?'

'We didn't just abandon them,' said Michael irritably. 'My mother lives with us. She's taking care of them.'

'Your mother? How fine a thing is filial piety. We should all return the love we are given. Have you seen Bellini's 'Virgin with Child' series in the Accademia?'

'Hardly. I've just arrived, remember?'

'Of course. But do go. They say so much about the relationship. One in particular I recall. The child stands supported by the Virgin's right arm which has grown six inches or so longer than the left, possibly to compensate for the desire, evident in her face, to push him off a balcony.'

'My God!' said Michael. 'You're sick!'

'Why so? Human relationships are always ambiguous, are they not? Have you never detested your mother? Deplored your children? Wished your wife dead and buried? Show me the man who has never rehearsed his demeanour at the funeral of those he loves most dearly and I will show you a monster.'

Long shot. A high exposed churchyard with the ground falling away sharply beyond the church wall to a rain-swept landscape.

In the foreground, umbrellas like foothills, down which stream cataracts of rain. The only sound the patter of the drops on the taut fabric and their hollower drumming on the coffin in the open grave.

Close-up. His own face, wet with what could be tears or just rain. The parson starts speaking, his monotonous voice merging with the drumming of the rain which now becomes real drumming and the voice a rhythmic orgiastic voodoo chant. Beside him stands his mother who turns sympathetically towards him and touches his arm reassuringly. But her hand is a claw which scrabbles and tears at the black plastic of his raincoat. In horror he pulls away, the mourners crowd close. He leaps into the grave. And falls like Alice, slowly tumbling through blackness towards . . .

Christ! I hammed from Hammer, he thought. Horror is not in graves and ghouls. It lives in glass and concrete hotels and in narrow Venetian streets and sits at café tables drinking with you. Which notion, he decided, was worse than his fantasy. *That* had been merely melodramatic, this was pretentious.

'I must go,' he said, finishing his icy beer too quickly for comfort.

'I'll walk a while with you,' said Dunkerley, rising also. He paid for the drinks from a plump Swiss-roll of notes which he kept in a leather pouch hung round his neck.

'Your postal order arrived then,' observed Michael.

'What?'

'Bunter.'

'Oh.'

Michael strode along energetically, but apart from the odd gasp, Dunkerley kept up with him easily.

'The worst thing is to run away from ourselves,' he said. 'Where do you want to go? I shall be your guide.'

'I doubt if I can afford you,' observed Michael.

'For a friend and a countryman, how should I charge? This way, this way. I see you are bent on making for the Accademia.'

After several minutes' stiff walking, which distinguished them from the slow tourist drift like piranha in an English lake, they reached the wooden bridge which Michael recalled passing beneath on the *vaporetto* that morning.

Here he halted and peered up the Grand Canal to where a trio of gondolas were moving with their strange lopsided smoothness round the bend which would take them up to the Ponte Rialto.

'See,' said Dunkerley, looking in the other direction, 'how finely the sun strikes on the domes of Santa Maria della Salute.'

Behind him Michael made a noise.

'Yes?' said Dunkerley.

'Nothing,' said Michael. But he had had his third brief glimpse of the afternoon. In one of the gondolas was a woman who he felt sure was Sarah; and she was not alone.

Sarah had finally made up her mind to have an affair. The moment of decision had come as Michael had left her at lunch. *Don't overdo it*, she had called after him in simple instinctive wifely admonition. He had looked back at her with an expression of vulnerable uncertainty which had touched her deeply. He thinks I'm getting at him, she realized guiltily. It was this feeling of guilt which had decided her to turn the imagined relationship into reality. If tenderness and pity could touch her now, so soon after what had happened, it would not be long before she would find herself confessing her innocence and perhaps even convincing him of it. A glimpse of a naked man in a shower – what meat for mockery that contained! No, only the real memory of another man's body inside her own could give her the moral strength to continue with Michael.

Besides it would give her something to talk about or at least hint at in an effort to counter the erotic confessions of her friend Avril. Perhaps she would even manage a long, juddering cry.

Her mind made up, she really wanted to get it over with as quickly as possible and had Aristide been available in the hotel, she felt quite capable of approaching him, arranging matters, and being ready to look at Venice within the hour. It had to be Aristide, of course. She was in credit there, and besides no one else available held the least attraction. She thought of Wilf and shuddered.

'He's a bastard,' said Wendy, sitting heavily beside her so that her large breasts juddered in her skimpy sun top.

Sarah started, wondering if she had been talking aloud.

'It's my money, you know.'

'What is?'

'Eight thousand quid I had when my dad died, what with the house and furniture and everything. Wilf was a back street butcher then. Half a pound of mince and a bone for the dog was a big order. Now he's got five shops. Two of them sell veal. Have you noticed what a funny smell this hotel's got?'

'Has it?'

'But the whole place stinks, doesn't it? Mind you, I'd been married to him three years then, so I knew a thing or two. There were papers signed. Are you going out? You're better in twos here. These greasy sods will snatch your bag or worse.'

'I've found most Italians perfectly pleasant and helpful.'

'Yes, I know. They're cunning with it. So there's nothing in a divorce for him. It'd be more worth my while.'

'Why don't you do it then?' asked Sarah. 'You've got grounds enough.'

'You mean the thumpings? I suppose so. Perhaps I will some day. What are we meant to look at in this place, do you know? I suppose it's all churches and statues.'

They strolled across St Mark's Square together, Wendy complaining bitterly about the unhygienic nature of pigeons and Sarah meditating on the monstrous stranglehold religion had applied for so long to human endeavour and social realization.

Their attempt to enter the basilica was thwarted by a strangely dressed man in a cocked hat and wearing a sword who appeared to take exception to Wendy's suntop.

'What's he want? Do I have to wear a hat?' asked Wendy replying to the beadle's gestures by placing the palm of her hand on her head.

'I don't think it's your head he's bothered about,' said Sarah.

'Sod him, then. I hate these damned churches anyway. It's too hot to walk. Let's take one of those silly boats.'

'A gondola? They're frightfully expensive, I believe.'

'My treat,' said Wendy. 'Come on. It's all down to Wilf's thumb on the scales.'

Her casual attitude to money did not extend to giving it away to work-shy foreigners, however. Sarah watched with mingled horror and admiration as Wendy, with no concessions whatever to the language barrier, negotiated with a brawny gondolier.

Matters reached an apparent deadlock which rapidly dissolved as the woman turned away with a bare-shouldered shrug worthy of a native.

'Where are we going?' asked Sarah as she scrambled aboard.

'God knows. I've told him to paddle around for an hour, that's all. But I've fixed the price.'

She looked ostentatiously at her watch as they set off and the gondolier rolled his eyes.

Of all the things she had done since coming on holiday, this made Sarah feel most decadent and socially parasitic. It was, she assured herself, just like taking a taxi. But taxis did not have tall, well-muscled men propelling them by main force while the passengers lay in cushioned comfort and drank in non-productive beauty on all sides.

In any case, taking taxis made her feel guilty too.

They went slowly up the Grand Canal, under the Academy Bridge, then turned up a side canal between two palazzi.

'Aren't they beautiful!' said Sarah.

'They must have rats,' said Wendy, nodding at the water washing up the steps almost to the very doors.

Thirty yards further along, the canal was spanned by a small hump-backed bridge on which stood one or two people, idly spectating.

'Hey, signora!' came a cry.

Sarah looked up and saw Aristide.

Her adulterous resolve had been forgotten in the pleasures of the voyage, but now it all came back to her and with it the thought how unattractive the youth looked.

As they passed beneath the bridge, Aristide jabbered away in Italian and when they emerged at the other side, the gondolier swung them in towards the bank and the boy leapt aboard.

'What the hell is this? A tram?' asked Wendy.

'Signora, forgive me. But when I see, I think how nice to speak with the English ladies once more.'

He sat down next to Wendy and grinned across at Sarah who felt embarrassed. It was not after all her gondola, but to point this out would imply that it was her company alone that had attracted Aristide to join them. She believed this to be true, though Aristide now began to direct most of his attention towards Wendy. Perhaps he recognizes the situation and is being diplomatic, she thought. But after a while she began to wonder if it was not merely that vast expanse of sun-flushed bosom which was capturing his interest. The thought piqued her more than she would have believed. She

examined the emotion with surprise. At least it boded well
for her act of adultery, always supposing she could offer
some counter-attraction.

From time to time Aristide spoke to the gondolier,
apparently collecting information which he then trans-
lated. Wendy, after her initial outburst, seemed reconciled
to his presence and even asked an occasional question.
Sarah began to feel rather left out of things, and taking
from her bag the Instamatic camera with which she
always hoped to get better photographs than Michael
from his absurdly expensive equipment, she began to snap
buildings and vistas.

They must have performed a circle on the side system,
for eventually they re-emerged into the Grand Canal and,
glancing at her watch, Sarah realized their hour was
almost finished.

Suddenly Aristide reached across and took the camera.

'Please,' he said. 'I take a picture of the signora. You
sit together. Good.'

He pulled Sarah into his place and crouched in the
middle of the gondola.

'No, wait. Signora Wendy, sit up please, the background must be right. Also the posture. Beautiful woman
must show her shape, no?'

Wendy didn't answer but looked rather flattered and
allowed Aristide to pull her from her cushion and seat
her on the gunwale. Sarah heard the gondolier say something to which Aristide replied dismissively.

'Now, beautiful woman, beautiful background. Is
good. Smile, please.'

Aristide crouched over the camera which Sarah realized,
again with considerable pique, was not including herself
in the shot at all.

'That is good. No. Wait, please. The hair falls over
your cheek. I fix.'

He reached forward as if to brush away an errant lock
from Wendy's cheek, lost his balance and fell heavily
against the side of the boat. The gondolier shouted as his
craft rocked violently. Wendy shrieked as she swayed
backwards over the water. Aristide made a desperate

H

lunge towards her, she grasped his arm, but it was too late. She had gone too far, and over the side she went, but with such a firm grip on the youth's arm that he followed her.

It was a sequence too swift to be taken in immediately, but with strong comic potential. Michael would have found it very funny, thought Sarah, especially the sight of Wendy's gipsy wig bobbing merrily to the surface a second before its owner.

Then she saw the *vaporetto*. It was coming at an angle across the canal to a landing point and the two figures struggling in the water lay directly in its path.

'Aristide!' shrieked Sarah.

The youth was the closer to the oncoming boat and seemed incapable of doing anything but tread water. Wendy suddenly put in a couple of powerful strokes, seized him by the neck of his shirt, forced herself high out of the water and dived.

The *vaporetto* passed over the circle of ripples she made only a second later. Then followed what seemed an endless moment while Sarah and everyone else scoured the murky surface of the canal with their eyes.

Suddenly the water erupted almost alongside the gondola.

'Give us a hand with this stupid bastard,' said Wendy grimly.

Apart from the loss of her wig and the destruction of her make-up Wendy had suffered comparatively little. Aristide had swallowed a fair quantity of water which gave Sarah some concern. Anyone who fell in an English canal and didn't have an immediate anti-everything injection could die within the hour, she remembered being told at a conservationist meeting. But Wendy assured her that continental standards of hygiene were so low that the few who survived infancy were immune for life.

The youth seemed to confirm this theory and was almost himself again by the time they reached their hotel. He kept on apologizing to Wendy for his clumsiness, though Sarah noticed he had not offered a word of regret

to herself for losing her camera. She felt inclined
to abandon him but when Wendy disappeared to her
room to get changed, she found she did not have the
heart.

'Those things need to be dried, not to mention cleaned,'
she said. 'You can borrow something of Michael's.'

'Please. No. I am OK. The sun is warm.'

'You will smell,' said Sarah. 'Don't be silly. Come on.'

She led him upstairs and produced a towel and a pair
of slacks which were getting too tight for Michael.

'I'll just find you a shirt,' she said, burrowing into a
drawer, 'and then you can dry yourself and get changed.'

When she looked up, she saw Aristide had anticipated
her. His jeans and tee-shirt lay at his feet and he was
unselfconsciously towelling himself. She felt that she had
been here before.

Sarah glanced at her watch. Wendy would be taking a
bath. She was almost certain Michael would not return
till dinner-time. Now seemed as good a time as any.

She smiled at the youth, who smiled back, but made no
move towards her. What should she do now? A subtle
move might be to say 'How hot it is in here!' and start
removing her blouse. But no! She rejected this as hypo-
critical and undignified. If a woman wanted a man, she
should indicate it honestly and unequivocally.

She went towards Aristide and handed him Michael's
shirt; then, taking his head in her hands, she gave him a
short kiss.

Next she reached down, grasped his penis and fell back
on the bed.

Unfortunately he showed no desire to fall with her.
Indeed he pulled away, which was not a wise move.

'Oh I'm so sorry, really I am!' said Sarah, aghast,
when his shriek subsided. 'Are you all right? Is there
anything I can do?'

He did not reply but, muttering angrily, he pulled on
the clothes she had given him, gathered up his own wet
things and made for the door. Here he paused to look
back at Sarah. 'Old,' he said. 'Useless,' he said. 'Women,'
he said.

The door crashed shut behind him.

Sarah sat on the bed and looked at herself in the mirror. The tears which began to run down her face belonged to another person with other hopes and other sorrows. She knew that. But all the same it was her face and to all outward appearances they were her tears.

Eventually they dried up and she lay down and fell asleep for a while. When she woke up, she washed her face and once more looked her normal capable and (so she was now convinced) totally unattractive self. But inside the tears still flowed.

Worst of all, though she had already locked and double-locked what had happened in the deepest cellar of her mind, she knew she had no capacity for wardership. Sooner or later she would turn the key and let it out, probably at the worst time to the worst person. Avril for instance; yes, it would probably be to Avril. It would be a cry for help, of course; a long juddering cry. 'Did you hear something dear?' 'Only a seagull on the wind.'

Of course, a pragmatist would console herself with the knowledge of the pleasure the story would give her friends. But this was a salve which fortune had not prescribed for Sarah.

Indeed, so deeply hurt was she that at first she felt almost grateful to be diverted by the news, brought hot-foot to her bedroom by an enthralled Wilf, that Michael had been arrested for murder.

II

'Am I under arrest?' asked Michael.

'No. Of course not,' said Captain Contarini.

'Then why are you holding me?'

'Because we want you to confess, of course. Why else?'

Captain Contarini had the expression of smiling, unassailable confidence which Michael recalled on the face of the police chief in Petri's *Investigation of a Citizen Above Suspicion*. Perhaps Captain Contarini himself was the murderer.

Exactly what the Captain's rank signified, indeed whether it was a police or some other kind of rank, Michael did not know. He presumed from the uniforms he had seen that he was in the hands of the P.S. rather than the Carabinieri, but nothing was certain. He needed something solid to get hold of.

'I'd like to see the British Consul,' said Michael.

'Of course you would. Unfortunately when we phoned, he was not available. Some committee for the preservation of Venice. You are not with Cook's?'

'No.'

'A pity. We could have got you a man from Cook's. You will have to tolerate my version of English, I'm afraid.'

'It's not a question of English,' said Michael. 'It's a question of representation.'

'Representation? What do you want with representation? I thought what you wanted was translation, because of my poor English,' said the captain in his almost immaculate Hollywood upper-crust English accent.

'The questions you're asking me are . . . suggestive,' said Michael carefully.

'How? Who is suggesting what? All we require is a little help. Just routine enquiries. Isn't that what they say?'

'It's not what they mean,' said Michael.

'Isn't it? You know English police methods then?'

'No. Just from television,' assured Michael.

'But you wanted to be represented too. That's significant.'

'Look,' protested Michael. 'Of course I want to be represented. You drag me away from my hotel, take my passport and tell me you want me to confess . . .'

'Ah, *confess*!' said Contarini, smiling broadly. 'I see. It is my poor English after all. I use the word religiously, of course. It is a semantic confusion. You are not Catholic, Mr Masson?'

'No,' said Michael, trying to work out what had just been said. 'I don't quite understand . . .'

'It is not easy,' agreed the captain seriously. 'So few of your countrymen really understand, even those who acknowledge the Pope.'

'I meant, I don't understand how your being a Catholic alters the way you use "confess" . . .'

'Catholic? Forgive me, you *are* confused,' said Contarini indignantly. 'I'm not Catholic. I am a good Communist. Mr Masson, please take off your clothes.'

'What!'

'It is just a formality.'

'It may be a formality to you,' said Michael, 'but to me it's a bloody liberty! What the hell's going on?'

'You have been awake all the time? You are not using drugs? No? Then how is it you do not know what is going on?'

'Now listen,' said Michael. 'I get back to my hotel. A gang of your policemen all fingering their guns like midnight in the dormitory tell me in broken English that you would like to talk to me about a murder. They more or less force me to come here. That's all I know about what's going on.'

'Which? *More*? Or *less*?'

'Sorry?'

'And *like midnight in the dormitory*? I do not know the idiom.'

'For God's sake, Captain. I only arrived in Venice at lunch-time. Since then, for most of the time, I've been in the company of someone I know. How the hell can I tell you anything about a murder?'

'Ah!' said Contarini, flashing the broad smile once more. 'Again it is a misunderstanding. It is not a murder in Venice we want to question you about!'

'Not a murder? Well, thank God for that,' said Michael with heartfelt relief. 'What is it then?'

'It is a murder in Rimini. Let us have some coffee.'

After leaving the hotel, he had been taken to a motor-boat which had proceeded to the Questura with scant regard for other craft or for the foundations of the buildings against which it sent barrage after barrage of waves. His confusion had been such that he had taken little notice of their route and it was only now that he really began to pay much attention to his immediate surroundings.

They were in a large room in much need of refurbishing. A once-beautiful desk stood between the captain and himself, but the leather top was torn, pieces of the marquetry decorations were missing and there were gaps also where sections of the ormolu mounts had been removed or knocked off. There was a carpet whose design had long since been trodden out of recognition. The wall hangings still retained a certain shabby elegance and a painting, darkened to a midnight scene by neglect, caught Michael's eye. While the captain went to the door and rattled out commands, he rose and looked more closely. There seemed to be four figures, one standing, the rest seated.

'The *Inquisitori* in the Palazzo Ducale,' said Contarini, returning to his desk.

'It needs cleaning.'

'No. Why? The English want to clean everything. That is why your consul is not with you now. It is probably a terrible painting, much improved by obscurity. Cigarette?'

He offered a packet of cigarettes, and waited till Michael went through his pockets and brought out a match-folder before producing a lighter in a leather pouch.

'You don't own a cigarette-lighter?' said the policeman.

'No. Not at the moment. I seem to have lost it. Or had it stolen.'

'Stolen? Yes. These holiday crowds attract the criminal element.'

He placed the lighter carefully on the desk. There was a knock at the door.

'Ah, coffee,' said Contarini, and went to admit a man with a tray.

Michael, as he guessed he was meant to do, picked up the lighter and turned it over in his hand. He recognized it without surprise.

'It's mine,' he said.

'I thought it was,' said Contarini cheerfully. 'M.O.M. Michael Oliphant Masson. *MOM* we thought at first. Mother. Or, from Mother. But that was our well-known maternal fixation leading us astray.'

'You are from the police in Rimini?'

'Yes, of course. But I am Venetian by birth. It was good to have an excuse to come home for a couple of days. Drink your coffee.'

Michael sipped and pondered.

'It's still not clear to me,' he said. 'Where did you get my lighter?'

'When we found it, I looked at the make. English. And the initials. Rimini is full of your countrymen, of course. Nevertheless, I set my men to checking registration lists at hotels. Those on that stretch of beach to start with, of course. Unfortunately I did not see the results till mid-morning, otherwise we could have talked before you left. But then I would not have had to come to Venice.'

He smiled, inviting Michael to share his appreciation of this good fortune.

'Where did you find it?'

'There was one good thumb-print on the lighter. Fortunately, your room had not been cleaned, or not very well cleaned. Not *cleaned* as the English like cleaning. We found prints, including the thumb-print. I presume it is yours, but we will check, of course. M.O.M. There were only three other *MOM*'s in thirty hotels. Fortunate, eh?'

'Please,' said Michael. 'Where did you find it?'

'Haven't I said? Beneath the body of a young man found dead on the beach at Rimini yesterday morning. Now, I have told you where we found it. Would you now please, Mr Masson, tell me where you lost it?'

Michael was confused. On the whole he felt that it would be easier to be guilty. Then at least you knew when and how to lie. Being innocent left you very vulnerable.

He ran through in his mind all the interrogation sequences he could recall, but the resultant montage of *Orphée*, *The Trial*, *The Cardinal*, *Ossessione* and *The Witches of Salem* did not help at all. Somehow the trials of Oscar Wilde kept on emerging as the dominant memory. It was odd, he reflected, how it is not necessarily the finest films which make the deepest impression.

'I can't remember,' he said. 'You see, if I'd known I was losing it, then probably I wouldn't have, would I?'

This was a test of the true quality of Contarini's English. He passed it with the merest wrinkle of concentration.

'Please tell me when first you noticed it was lost.'

'Oh, two, three days ago. I can't remember.'

'Did you mention this to anyone?'

'I don't think so.'

'You did not ask at the reception desk in your hotel, for instance? Or even think of informing the police?'

'No. I mean, I didn't really think it was lost. Just mislaid. I'm very careless with things.'

'I see. Have you any theory how your lighter should have come into the possession of the murdered man?'

'One moment,' said Michael cunningly. 'You did not actually say it was in his possession, did you? I thought you said it had been found by the body.'

'Beneath.'

'Beneath, then. I may have lost it on that part of the beach earlier in the week. Were the man's prints on it?'

'Perhaps,' said Contarini. 'It is difficult to say. There is much blurring, except for the one thumb-print. Yours.'

'You *think* it's mine,' said Michael. It was remarkable

how cool he was feeling. He was already rehearsing versions of the story to recount back at the hotel, and later home in England.

'Alternatively, the murdered man may have been a thief, a pickpocket. I suppose you have identified him?'

'Yes. He is Guido Falcone, a student. His family have a small painting business on the outskirts of Rimini. Very respectable people. There has been no trouble with the police.'

Michael shrugged his shoulders expressively.

'With young people, there has to be a start.'

'You are a cynic, Mr Masson. Tell me, what were you doing the evening before last?'

'Well, that's easy. I spent the day touring in a car with some friends. We ended up in Florence, got back to the hotel about two o'clock in the morning and went to bed.'

'Names, please. Your friends. Anyone you saw when you returned.'

He noted them down carefully and examined the list.

'Your wife did not go with you?'

'No. But as I told you, she was in the hotel lounge when I returned.'

'Very touching,' said Contarini seriously. He went to the door again and shouted. A uniformed officer entered.

'Mr Masson, please go with this man. Firstly you will have the fingerprints taken. Then you will be medically examined. It will take only twenty minutes at the most. It is of course purely voluntary, but I am sure you will co-operate. I shall see you again before you return to your hotel.'

He glanced at his watch and smiled ruefully.

'Soon it will be your dinner-time. I hope the food is good, real Venetian.'

It was this comfortable note which made Michael hold back his protests and follow the officer.

Contarini spoilt things by sticking his head out of the door and shouting after him, 'These clothes you are wearing, did you have them on that night?'

He had to think hard.

'No,' he said.

'What were you wearing.'

'A pair of whipcord slacks and a chocolate-brown towelling shirt.'

'Whipcord? Good.'

The door slammed and Michael continued on his way.

An hour later the captain appeared at the door of the small bare room in which Michael was sitting naked except for a blanket over his shoulder.

'Here are your clothes,' said Contarini. He tossed shirt, trousers and beach shoes to Michael and continued to examine what seemed to be a fascinating sheet of paper in his hand.

'These aren't what I had on when I came here,' protested Michael. 'Nothing was said about taking my clothes away. This is outrageous!'

'I'm sorry. We must check, you understand. Your wife sent you these.'

'Sarah? You've seen Sarah? Where is she?'

'At the hotel. I sent one of my men to talk with her. Don't worry. My officer assures me they serve dinner till eight-thirty, nine o'clock if you don't mind it being a bit cold. We are civilized in Venice. By the way, something unfortunate has happened.'

Michael felt very alarmed.

'To Sarah? What, for God's sake? Look, I want to get out of here!'

He began pulling on the trousers. They felt odd without underpants, but Contarini's minion had not brought any new ones and his old ones were God knows where.

'No, nothing like that. It is only that we wanted your whipcord slacks and brown towelling shirt. That's right? Well, it seems your wife has given them away.'

Michael stopped with his trousers round his thighs.

'Given them away?' he repeated disbelievingly.

'Yes. To a friend. A Frenchman. Aristide. She did not know his second name. You know this man?'

'Yes. To Aristide! But they were my favourite slacks!'

'Perhaps you can tell us his second name.'

'I don't know the bastard's second name!' protested Michael, resuming his dressing.

'A close friend, I understood.'

'No friend at all of mine. I saw him for the first time three days ago. God, what was she thinking of?'

'This is very odd. Your wife gives away your favourite clothes to a Frenchman whose name you do not know and whom you met only three days ago? This is very awkward, Mr Masson. For you I mean. How shall we find this man?'

'Well,' said Michael, 'for a start he'll be wearing a brown shirt and whipcord slacks. And as for it being odd, I assure you the streets of shanty towns from the Bosphorus to the Yellow Sea are full of happy natives whom I have never met in my life, and each and every one of them is wearing my clothes!'

'Ah!' said Contarini. 'I understand. Mrs Masson is generous of spirit, is this what you are saying? What a pity it should have been these particular clothes she gave away. Never mind. Just one more thing before you go and enjoy your dinner, Mr Masson. I have here the doctor's report. You should take more exercise, I think. For a man of your age, this blood pressure . . . well, I swim two kilometres each day, you know. But it is not that. No. These lacerations on your neck and shoulders, I saw them myself just now as you dressed, the doctor is not quite clear what they are. Perhaps . . .'

'What? Oh, those. Well, it's a bit awkward,' said Michael. 'They are, well, scratches. From fingernails.'

'Yes, so the doctor surmised. But how . . .?'

'I shouldn't have thought a genuine hot-blooded Venetian would need to see the rushes, Captain! They are the marks of passion, what else?'

'So! Well, I see. You are to be congratulated, Mr Masson. Forgive me, but it may be necessary to confirm. With your permission, I shall ask a female officer to speak with your wife.'

'My wife?'

'Yes, your wife.' Contarini looked at him with a faint smile. 'I know the English have much modesty on such matters. My officer will be discreet. Your wife will confirm what you say, I am sure. Will she not, Mr Masson?'

Michael fastened his shoes slowly.

'In a manner of speaking, yes. Unfortunately, well . . . look does it matter? I mean, to tell the truth, you're . . .'

Michael pulled himself up short, horrified. He'd been going to say, 'you're a man of the world.' What kind of line was that for a cultured man to speak? He was behaving like . . . his mind spun round, seeking an identity to discard.

'Yes, Mr Masson?'

'It wasn't my wife.'

'Ah.'

The monosyllable was totally neutral.

'Does it matter?'

'Not to me, Mr Masson.'

'No, I mean, is it important? For Christ's sake, what difference does it make if I have a few scratches on my back?'

'Where did you get them, Mr Masson.'

'In Florence if you must know.'

'That same night?'

'Yes.'

'Whereabouts in Florence?'

'How should I know?'

'All right. With whom?'

'I don't know. Maria, I think. Or Carla.'

Now Contarini did look surprised.

'There were two?'

'Yes. Is that enough for you, Captain?'

'Witnesses are only useful if we can find them, Mr Masson.'

'If it's witnesses you want, there were three other people there. You have their names.'

'Your companions? You were together.'

'All the time. Look, Captain, I'm not certain how the law works in Italy. My only acquaintance with it is through the cinema and that can be misleading. But I think unless I can now return to my hotel, I should insist on having someone from the Consulate here, even if it's only the cleaner.'

'Through the cinema? You are a movie fan? I also,' said Contarini, with a look of pleasure. 'I will take you back to the hotel now and we will talk about films on the way. You should be here for the Festival, not now when there is nothing but tourists everywhere. Now, our Italian cinema, what do you think of it?'

'I think it's superb,' said Michael, feeling diverted again but glad to be so. 'Always advancing. Fellini is my favourite director.'

'Fellini? Yes, I see. It is good to hear you say it. But I wonder, do you think we can ever produce someone like Fred Astaire?'

As they left, Contarini put his arm across Michael's shoulders and executed a few tap-steps. The policeman on duty outside saluted and grinned broadly. Michael felt more threatened than at any time since he had arrived in the building.

At the hotel the guests were well into dinner and Contarini left him in the foyer, urging him to enjoy his meal. The policeman had talked of little save Fred Astaire and Ginger Rogers on the return journey, and Michael suspected he was trying some subtle Latin ploy for establishing a relationship between hunter and hunted. Such things were not unknown. He searched his mind for examples. Surely someone had filmed *Crime and Punishment*? But all that he kept getting were flashes of innocent men being wrongly condemned. Renoir's *La Chienne*, also *La Bête Humaine*; Hitchcock's *The Wrong Man*. Oshima's *Death by Hanging*. No. He *had* done it.

The seating here was much more informal than at the Leonardo, and, as though moved by some atavistic need for propinquity, Wendy, Wilf, Bob, Molly, Sarah and the ubiquitous Dunkerley had joined two tables together. Michael was slightly put out to see Sarah tucking into a pork cutlet, but she compensated by rising to her feet when she saw him and crying, 'Oh, Michael!' as though he had just returned from the dead. Indeed, so enthusiastic and excited were they all by his appearance that after a while he began to feel rather amazed to be there at all and he found himself making non-committal, half-humorous replies to their questions, like Danny Kaye's

RAF ace in *The Secret Life of Walter Mitty*.

'Give the man room!' cried Wilf finally. 'Here you are, Mike, a spot of the old vino. I expect you need it.'

He took the glass gingerly but was relieved to find that someone other than Wilf had chosen the wine; of those assembled, probably Dunkerley. He nodded gratefully at the fat man even though he suspected he was eating his dinner.

'What's happened?' said Sarah anxiously. 'I've been worried out of my wits. They came and took some of your clothes. Wilf rang the British Consulate for me, but they were all out at some meeting about preserving Venice. You'd think there was enough to do here in the way of slum clearance and health benefits without asking for thousands of pounds to clean some statues!'

'It's all been a mistake,' assured Michael. 'It was about that body they found on the beach in Rimini. Apparently my lighter was found nearby . . .'

'Nearby?' interrupted Bob. 'How near's that?'

'Well, very close. Underneath, in fact. But it doesn't really matter . . .'

'Sounds as if it matters a bloody lot to me,' said Bob.

'I meant, it doesn't matter to me personally,' said Michael with some acerbity. 'I had mislaid the lighter some days previously. Some of you may have heard me mention it.'

He paused. There was the kind of silence which follows a request for volunteers in the Army.

'Did you know this man, the one who was killed?' asked Bob.

'No, of course not. I mean, I haven't seen him, of course. But I didn't know his name.'

'You say they took some of your clothes?'

'Yes. What I was wearing today. They brought these for me to change into.'

'They wanted your whipcord slacks and towelling shirt,' said Sarah suddenly. 'But I loaned them to Aristide.'

This was another conversation-stopper.

'He fell in the water,' explained Sarah defiantly. 'I couldn't let him go out wearing wet clothes.'

'That little bastard tried to drown me,' asserted Wendy, who was smoking between courses again.

'No,' protested Sarah. 'It was an accident.'

'Some accident. And he didn't fall in, I pulled him in,' she added triumphantly. 'I should have let the water-bus mince him!'

'My missus always had a talent for the dramatics,' interposed Wilf.

'How was this Italian killed?' asked Bob.

'I don't know,' said Michael. 'I never thought to ask.'

'I should if I were you,' said Bob heavily. 'Or else they might think you don't need to.'

'Oh, be quiet, Bob!' said Molly. 'It's all been a simple mistake, that's obvious.'

Michael looked at her in surprise, less at her support than at the manner of it. Three days earlier he wouldn't have put money on Molly's addressing Bob without written permission, let alone treating him in this dismissive fashion. Something had happened to her. He hoped Bob didn't imagine it had anything to do with him. She certainly looked very attractive now, faintly flushed, with a new purpose in her eyes, as though she had had some significant experience. He felt a sudden desire to reach out his hand beneath the table and thrust it up her skirt. Would her expression change? He wasn't about to find out, though. He felt himself sweating in fear of Bob's reaction to the mere thought and held his glass tightly in both hands while his mind ran through various under-table shots. The Marx Brothers had done it, of course; Danny Kaye (that great wasted talent) also; Chaplin? Perhaps, but where? Lemmon and Curtis in *Some Like It Hot* . . .

'Of course it is a mistake,' agreed Dunkerley magisterially. 'One of the great frontier-transcending forces of all ages has been the stupidity of the police.'

'Your side-kick trying to drown me was no mistake,' said Wendy darkly. 'I hope these police aren't stupid enough to let him run around free.'

'Come now,' said Dunkerley rather sadly. 'Aristide is but a child, a young man gaining experience of life. Never wish such a one into the rude hands of the law.'

'They'll want him anyhow,' said Wilf. 'If they want Mike's clothes. You could ingratiate yourself a bit there, Syd, old son. Go and find a policeman and tell him where you and Ari are staying.'

'I am, of course, eager to perform my civic duty and support the law,' said Dunkerley. 'Unfortunately I cannot help in this instance.'

'Oh? Why's that?'

'Aristide and I are not sharing lodgings in Venice.'

'What's a matter? Had a tiff?' said Wilf with a grin.

'You might say that,' said Dunkerley, regarding him fixedly. 'A policy disagreement would be a better description, I think.'

'Oh, I *am* sorry,' said Sarah.

A waiter arrived and started removing dishes. Michael rose.

'Please finish your dinner,' he said. 'I'm not very hungry. It's been a long day. I think I'll try to get some sleep.'

Sympathetic grunts ran round the table like a *feu de joie*, misfiring only at Bob. As he went through the foyer, Michael glanced at the hotel's main door open against the still heavy heat. Leaning there smoking a cigarette and looking dreadfully bored was a policeman. For the first time in his life, Michael felt really homesick.

Sarah had watched him go with a heart full of worry. It seemed best to leave him alone for a while. He looked as if he needed to be left alone. Besides she wanted to sample one of the delicious looking ice confections she had noticed served at a nearby table.

Dunkerley poured himself another glass of the wine which he had insisted on contributing to the meal. He had turned up just before dinner and had been at the same time so concerned and so comforting when given the news of Michael's arrest that it would have been churlish not to invite him to stay and eat. Besides, that unity in the face of disaster which the English are so proud of required feeding with informed hypotheses. But with Michael's return, the all-clear seemed to have been sounded and it was time to revert to type.

'I realize, Mrs Masson,' he said, 'that you perhaps do not feel like an excursion, but I do have a fairly intimate knowledge of Venice and should any of the rest of you desire to plunge into Venetian night life, I would be charmed to guide you.'

Wilf looked at him speculatively; Bob snorted; Molly glanced at her husband as though contemplating testing her new-found strength by a unilateral acceptance of the offer. Only Wendy spoke.

'If you think I'm letting you lead me down these nasty little alleyways where your boy-friend might be lurking, you must be mad!'

Wilf laughed at this.

'Perhaps another night, Sydney,' he said. 'We're all a bit knackered, I think. I'll just try a couple in the bar, perhaps take a stroll to St Mark's to say my prayers, then it's me for bed. How's that for virtuous!'

The confections turned out to be rather disappointing, evaporating rather than melting in the mouth. Afterwards Wilf and Dunkerley announced they wouldn't have coffee and set off for the bar. Bob vacillated for a moment, but was no match for the combined wills of three women and left ponderously.

Watching him go was like seeing an aged general who has come to believe the myth of his own invincibility suddenly scenting the putrid stench of defeat for the first time. Sarah had been delighted to see the signs of insurgency in Molly's behaviour and would have liked to believe that her own encouragement had contributed largely to the change. She certainly felt enough responsibility to want to warn Molly that the battle was far from over. Just as she herself had been postponing the final struggle with Michael till they were back on familiar territory (though, somehow, the fiasco with Aristide had spiked some of her guns more than the actual getting-even of consummation would have done), so she felt Bob was the kind of man who'd prefer to have his back to his own fireplace rather than some foreign wall. The public-ness of a holiday disadvantaged him. At home with the children as his allies, Molly might find herself outgunned.

She was wondering how she could sound this warning note with Wendy present when the latter spoke.

'If I were you I should leave him.'

Molly and Sarah looked at each other unable to guess through the swirl of tobacco smoke who was being addressed.

'I don't mean here. When we get back. Just get in a taxi and go. Don't say anything. Just do it.'

'I'm sorry, but . . .' began Sarah.

'I should have done it years ago. Years. It might be too late. You, you've got youth on your side.'

It was Molly who was meant, decided Sarah regretfully.

'Youth is a doubtful ally, my dear.'

Dunkerley had returned, soft-footed, to collect his cigarettes from beside his plate. He smiled seriously at Wendy.

'Frequently it proves a coward,' he continued. 'And in the end it is inevitably a deserter. Look around you. The world is full of people who have all had youth on their side and yet it has not prevented any of them from arriving at their present sad defeats. Mrs Masson, I wonder if I might have a private word.'

Puzzled, Sarah rose and followed the fat man to the far side of the now almost empty dining-room. He leaned against the foyer door and looked embarrassed.

'The real reason I came to the hotel this evening was to speak with you, but the distressing news about your husband naturally relegated my own intentions. However, all seems well now, so perhaps I should speak. When I was with Michael earlier this afternoon . . .'

'He was with you?' interrupted Sarah in surprise.

'We ran into each other,' said Dunkerley. 'We had a long chat. I got the impression from something he said that he felt Aristide was paying too much attention to you.'

'Did you? I should have thought you got that impression from eavesdropping on the coach this morning,' said Sarah acidly.

'I did sense an undercurrent,' said Dunkerley with a show of reluctance. 'Then after Michael and I parted – I can only spend so much time in the Accademia without being overcome – I met Aristide.'

'I thought you had fallen out,' interposed Sarah.

'Yes, yes, we have. It was . . . after this meeting,' said Dunkerley. 'He told me about the accident on the canal. I asked him about the clothes he was wearing. I knew they were not his, I am fairly intimate with his wardrobe. He became evasive, I pressed him. He grew angry. I persevered.'

Sarah felt herself flushing. Dunkerley took her arm and pressed it sympathetically. She pulled herself away.

'Forgive me,' he said, 'but I feel a responsibility for the boy. In a sense, I am *in loco parentis*. His mother, a devout lady of good family who married beneath her, made me promise to keep a quasi paternal eye on him. Indeed I believe that were it not for my own imminence when he first set out on this poor man's Grand Tour, she would have stopped at nothing to prevent it. You look surprised. He was barely eighteen then and provincial France is a stronghold of the traditional family virtues. Authority would have supported her.'

'I was looking surprised at the difference between his version of making your acquaintance and your own,' said Sarah.

Dunkerley chuckled and shook his head.

'So. So. A romancer is our Aristide! Too young to have done enough to make him an object of interest, or so he believes, he falls back on invention. What was it – the Algerian brothel or the Marseilles gaol?'

'The gaol,' admitted Sarah.

'Indeed? Well, we passed through Marseilles it is true, and took a cup of coffee within sight of the prison roofs – it was a particularly clear day. Ah, youth, youth!'

'You didn't seem to think much of it a minute ago.'

'Nor do I. It is a time of self-deception and, worse, insensitivity to others. When I heard what had happened . . .'

'What did Aristide tell you?' asked Sarah, wondering

how on earth she had got into this conversation. It was, as Michael might have said, like the script of a British 'B' film about Scotland Yard – bad, but with an almost enjoyable inevitability.

'He told me that you made him an offer which most normal young men would have found it hard to refuse.'

'Normal?'

'Come now, Sarah,' said Dunkerley indulgently. 'You must have spotted my drift by now. Aristide is, of course, homosexual. Fond of the company of women, but nothing more. I'm sorry.'

He was looking over her shoulder as if to save her the embarrassment of a full-frontal stare. Abruptly he patted her elbow and said, 'There, there,' then turned and walked away towards the bar.

Sarah watched him go, feeling angry and stupid. Even the repressed Molly had seen at a glance what kind of sexual animal Aristide was. *Jane* she had called him. Oh damn! Well, at least it made the ghastly episode a mistake rather than a failure. Avril would make a hilarious anecdote out of it. After all, basically it was just another comic queer story, a genre which, like Irish jokes, Paki jokes and sick jokes, she deplored but which still occasionally caught her unawares and made her smile. But not this one. Oh no. Avril had the track record to be able to admit the occasional fiasco, but Sarah was not about to confess to having fallen in the Maiden Stakes. Oh God, what a metaphor! It was time she joined the others.

'Signora Masson? Perhaps I could occupy a moment of your time.'

She turned. Standing in the foyer door was a tall, dark man in a blue suit. He was extremely attractive but she promised herself he would need to produce a wife and four kids before she responded to his attractiveness.

'I am Captain Contarini,' he said. 'The manager pointed you out. I was waiting till you finished your conversation.'

That explained why Dunkerley had moved off so abruptly, thought Sarah. Nothing about this charming man said 'policeman' to her, but then recent experience had revealed just how insensitive her people responses were.

'My husband is resting, Captain. I would prefer that he should not be disturbed.'

'Of course. Shall we sit down?'

They sat at one of the dining-room tables and Contarini offered her a cigarette from a gold case. She shook her head and he put the case away without taking one himself, a demonstration of good manners which her feminist studies had taught her to mistrust.

'Was the meal good?' enquired Contarini, playing with a cruet.

'Quite good.'

'Your husband, did he enjoy it?'

'He didn't eat anything. Understandably, he was fatigued.'

'But he must eat! A man needs his strength.'

Contarini sounded genuinely upset.

'How can I help you, Captain?' said Sarah.

'Oh, it is nothing really. This man, Aristide, that you loaned your husband's shirt to. You told my officer you did not know his whereabouts?'

'That's right.'

'I see. He moves in the company of an Englishman, Sydney Dunkerley, I gather. Was it by chance Mr Dunkerley you were just talking with?'

A sudden fear struck Sarah that he had been standing close enough to the open door to overhear all their conversation.

'Yes.'

'I see. I must talk with him soon.'

'I doubt if he can help,' said Sarah quickly. 'He doesn't know where Aristide is living.'

'Ah,' said Contarini, looking at her keenly. 'You have enquired? I see. Tell me, Signora, the day your husband went to Florence, what time did the party return?'

'I'm not sure. About two, I think. I was still up, I'd been having a drink with my friends and we didn't really notice the time.'

She nodded towards her 'friends', Molly and Wendy,

who were regarding the interview with undisguised interest.

'And then?'

'Well, we went to bed.'

'Immediately?'

Sarah thought for a moment.

'No. Not immediately.'

'I see. Did anyone go out after the men returned?'

'No. Well, yes. Mr Dunkerley went. He wasn't staying in our hotel, you see.'

'Alone.'

'Yes. Well, no. Michael stepped out with him.'

'Ah. For how long would you say?'

'I don't know. A moment, that's all.'

'A moment. You mean a few seconds?'

'No. Longer than that.'

'Some minutes then? Five? Ten? Longer?'

'I wasn't looking at my watch,' said Sarah, adding in a real English lady's voice she did not know she possessed, 'If that is all, Captain, I think I should join my husband.'

'Of course,' said Contarini, jumping up. He really was a very attractive man, thought Sarah, unable to resist returning his smile.

'But I must not forget my second question,' continued the policeman. 'Please, do you recognize this man?'

He produced a photograph of a good-looking youth with a shock of black hair. There were marks at each corner which showed it had been removed from a frame.

'I don't think so,' said Sarah.

'You're sure?'

'Well, it's hard to say. So many boys here . . .'

'. . . look the same,' Contarini concluded for her. 'You cannot tell us apart, like sheep and Chinamen.'

'I didn't mean that,' protested Sarah. 'Who is it?'

'Who do you think?' said Contarini brutally. 'Thank you, Signora.'

'I didn't realize,' she told Michael a few minutes later. 'Somehow I thought that a dead man's picture would be like a death-mask. I'm so stupid. They must have got it from his home. Oh, his poor mother!'

'What's Contarini doing now?' asked Michael. He was lying fully clothed on the bed. The room was full of cigarette smoke, but for once Sarah did not protest.

'He went over to Wendy and Molly as I came away.'

'What does he want to talk to them for?'

'I've no idea,' said Sarah. 'I hope Wendy doesn't start on that daft business about Aristide again.'

'Him!' sneered Michael. 'What's so daft about that?'

'Oh, come on, Michael. I know you don't like the boy, but he's got no reason to try to drown Wendy!'

'No? Well, listen to this. The day we went to Florence, Dunkerley told me Wilf had asked what he would charge for killing his wife.'

'What? That's absurd! I mean, why?' Sarah was amazed.

'Why what? Why kill her? Or why Dunkerley?'

'Both.'

'If you were Wilf, wouldn't you want rid of her? And along comes Dunkerley, saying he's an ex-mercenary, a soldier who hires himself out.'

Sarah shook her head.

'I can't believe it,' she said emphatically. 'It's like something out of one of those stupid thriller films you try to pretend are Art. I can't believe it.'

'Why not?' asked Michael, piqued by this attack on his taste. 'You readily accept any atrocity story that comes out of the half-dozen countries whose economy you try to undermine every time you go shopping. What's so difficult to believe about an Englishman being willing to pay to get rid of his wife? He was merely putting into words what tens of thousands must think every day.'

'Including you?'

'Including me, yes!' snapped Michael, rolling over on the bed so that he faced away from her.

She glared down at his back and wished with all her heart she could be having the comforting thought that only a few hours ago she had committed adultery on this very blanket.

III

The following morning Michael found that the management had set its seal of approval on the desire for togetherness evinced by the three families the previous night and the two tables pushed together were now covered by a single cloth.

Wilf was there already, drinking coffee, and opposite him sat Molly toying with a bread roll.

'Hello, Mike,' said Wilf. 'I was telling Molly here about this teachers' training place that comes under my jurisdiction. Big intake of mature students. Now, you're in the racket already so perhaps you can help. What's a teacher get paid these days? I ought to know but I never had a head for figures.'

'I've no idea. Couple of thousand. I'm on a different scale,' said Michael.

'Are you really? Like me when I'm weighing Christmas turkeys! Well, I never knew that. I must tell them that on the Committee when I get home.'

'You mean they won't know?' said Molly, wide-eyed.

'Now I didn't say that,' said Wilf seriously. 'Don't think I'm implying that no one on the Committee's got a grasp of figures. Oh no. Some of 'em can't read either!'

He roared with laughter, reached across the table and patted Molly's hand. Michael admired the way in which she maintained an expression of emotional neutrality, only a slight flicker of the eyelids showing the revulsion she must be feeling. He almost wished Bob would arrive at this moment and vent some of his jealous violence on this braying jackass.

'I must love you and leave you,' said Wilf, noisily emptying his coffee cup. 'Things to do, things to do. You get Mike to fill in the details, my dear. It's a grand life if you like kids and you're a bit mad, eh Mike? Cheerioh, Molly. Goodbye, Mr Chips!'

Michael watched him go with relief.

'The great thing about holiday friendships,' he said, 'is that they come to an end.'

'That's not a very nice thing to say,' observed Molly.

'No, I'm sorry. Of course I didn't mean . . .' He broke off and grinned his boyish youthful grin.

'Are you serious about doing a teacher's training course?' he asked.

'Why not?'

'No reason,' he said. 'If it's what you want, I think it's a great idea. I really don't know much about teacher training, but I do have to interview prospective students for my department from time to time, and if it would help, I could give you a few pointers.'

He became aware that Molly's gaze was missing his face by six inches to the left and three feet upwards. He glanced round. It was of course Bob.

'Good morning,' he said brightly. To his surprise Bob did not glower threateningly as was his wont but instead nodded towards the door.

'You're wanted,' he said, stressing the second word.

Michael looked. Standing by the door wearing a light grey suit of impeccable cut and the smiling self-assurance of Cary Grant was Contarini.

'Excuse me,' he said to Molly, and rose.

Contarini was full of apologies for this early call.

'I must return to Rimini soon, you understand. That is where the key to the mystery lies. This has been the slightest diversion. But you have had no breakfast I perceive? Nor have I. Let us sit here in the quiet corner and I am sure the management will be kind.'

He snapped his fingers. A waiter immediately abandoned the people he was serving and approached. Contarini said a few words and a pot of coffee and some fresh rolls were skilfully diverted to their table.

'I should begin by saying how charming and co-operative all the members of your group have been. So often visitors, especially from the great democracies like your own, become so aggressive in the face of official questions. But not these. You have met some nice people on your holiday, Mr Masson.'

'Well,' said Michael. 'Yes. I suppose I have.'

'Another roll? Good, aren't they? Yes, your friends were very forthcoming. More than you were, it seems, Mr Masson.'

'What?' Michael felt alarmed. For God's sake, what had they been saying?

'Have you ever seen this man?'

He looked down at the photograph which he assumed was the one shown to Sarah. The face smiled up at him, but the eyes were dark and shadowed.

'I don't know. It's faintly familiar but . . .'

'Could it be the youth you had the brawl with at the hotel barbecue? Or the one who addressed you in the Piazza Tre Martiri in Rimini?'

'What? Christ, they *have* been talking, haven't they! No, I don't think . . . I'm not sure. Look, is this the dead youth?'

Contarini regarded him steadily through the steam from the coffee-cup he held in both hands before his lips.

'You do not know? Yes. It is he, Mr Masson.'

Michael laughed in relief.

'Then it can't be the same.'

'Why?'

'Well, the boy at the barbecue – and it wasn't a brawl, Captain, merely a slight awkwardness – is alive and well. I saw him in Venice only yesterday.'

Contarini expressed no surprise but rose and bowed. Looking round, Michael saw that Sarah had come into the dining-room. She paused uncertainly, gave a nervous smile in acknowledgement of Contarini's greeting and continued on her way to join Bob and Molly. Michael watched her go with a feeling which he identified with a slight raising of his rational eyebrows as betrayal. This holiday had changed her in some hard-to-define way. Only a few days ago their relationship had been normal – that was to say, she caused him a great deal of irritation but he always felt in control. Now somehow a rein had slipped. His attempts to apply the old verbal curbs seemed to be quite ineffective. Had sleeping with Aristide been such a life-changing experience? Perhaps it was the start

of something new. Perhaps it heralded a move into the
local wife-swopping set when they got home. The thought
filled him with distaste. Adultery was like making a film;
the pleasure was commensurate with the skill of the
deceit; for technically speaking, film was nothing but
ocular deceit. This was why he had always ignored the
tempting charms of Avril-with-the-long-juddering-cry.
She would be incapable of discretion. You'd need a sound-
proof room to start with. But apart from that, she was as
thick as a plank. Like a classical metamorphosis in
reverse, a tree turned into a nymph!

'Something amuses you, Mr Masson!'

'What? Oh no. I'm sorry. I was day-dreaming.'

'And this boy you saw in Venice, was this perhaps a
day-dream too?'

'No!' he protested indignantly. 'I saw him.'

'Why should he be in Venice, Mr Masson?'

'I don't know. I felt, well, I know it sounds silly, but I
felt he was following me.'

He glared defiantly at Contarini who did not meet his
gaze.

'Mr Dunkerley mentioned this boy you claim you saw.'

'There you are then,' said Michael, 'I didn't make him
up.'

'Mr Dunkerley did not see the boy himself, he says. But
he understood from what you said that *you* were pursuing
him.'

'That's right. I saw him in the Piazza San Marco and
thought he looked familiar. So . . .'

Contarini silenced him with a movement of the hand.

'I understood you to say he was in Venice because *he*
was following *you*, Mr Masson?'

'Yes. I did. But, I mean, well, he must have known I'd
spotted him, I suppose.'

'But why, Mr Masson? What was there in this – what
did you call it? – *awkwardness* to make this youth follow
you to Venice? Mrs Trueman says that while being
grateful for your chivalrous intentions, she felt you over-
reacted to the situation.'

'Did she?' Michael was indignant.

'You sound reproachful. But she showed her gratitude, did she not?'

'What the hell does that mean?'

'Did you not make love to her?'

'*No!*'

'No? Were you never then in her bedroom with her, in the middle of the night, naked?'

'No, I wasn't. Well, yes, in a sense. Did she say . . .? No. I know!'

He glared angrily down the room at Bob who was watching the interview impassively.

'It's a misunderstanding, Captain. I was merely trying to be helpful. Mr Lovelace has misread what he saw, not without malice, I feel.'

'Really? But he was hardly malicious in his description of what happened in Florence.'

'What did he say?'

'That in the house of the signora you and he merely spectated at some form of erotic performance, he from choice, you because you seemed to be too drunk.'

'That's monstrous!' proclaimed Michael, feeling himself swell with what could only be called unrighteous indignation. 'I know when I've . . . you saw the scratches!'

'Yes. I did. Why should Mr Lovelace lie to me?'

'He's jealous! That's why. He thinks I'm making a play for his wife.'

'Are you?'

'No. Of course not! Why should I?'

Contarini shrugged.

'She is an attractive woman. And you by your own admission are a hot-blooded man. Except perhaps when lying naked on a bed with someone else's wife, or so you claim.'

'Think what you will,' said Michael obstinately. 'If you're any kind of policeman, you'll discount anything Lovelace says about me.'

'Strange,' said Contarini. 'It is just because I am a policeman that I have taken everything he says more seriously than almost anyone else.'

'Why's that?'

'Did you not know?' he asked, surprised. 'Mr Lovelace is a policeman also.'

'Well, well, well,' said Michael. 'So that's it. I never really believed he was a brain surgeon.'

He looked at Bob again. He seemed to have finished his breakfast but was clearly not going to move while there was anything to watch.

'What else has he told you?' he asked.

'Nothing. But his wife . . .'

'What's she had to say? Nothing that supports her husband's mad allegations, I'm sure.'

'She seems to recollect that when you escorted Mr Dunkerley from the hotel in the early hours of that morning, you did not return for twenty-five perhaps thirty minutes.'

'What? But that's absurd! I came straight back. My wife will tell you.'

'Mrs Masson was uncertain.'

'Was she indeed! Well, Dunkerley then. I talked to him by the swimming pool – he was dossing down in a beach-chair for the night – and I left him after only a minute.'

'Yes, he confirms that.'

'There you are then!'

'But he is not certain which direction you took.'

'Oh God,' said Michael. 'So that's it. I'm supposed to have walked two hundred yards up the beach, met, murdered and concealed this boy, and got back to the Leonardo all in half an hour.'

'It is possible.'

'Motive?'

'Who knows? Our surgeon has a theory that some form of sexual embrace took place.'

'Ah, the scratches!'

'Perhaps.'

'But I'm the well-known womanizer, remember?'

Contarini shrugged.

'In the two cases where you are accused, you hotly deny it. In the one case where you claim it, you are contradicted. In any case, perhaps the dying spasms of a young man with a knife in his belly could cause such marks.'

'Oh Christ.'

Michael took out his cigarettes, Contarini offered him a light. He was using Michael's lighter.

'The lighter!' said Michael. 'I've remembered the last time I had it. It was the night of the barbecue. Perhaps I lost it then when I was helping Mrs Trueman. The boy could have picked it up. That would explain how it came to be in his possession!'

'Hardly, Mr Masson,' said Contarini. 'Not if you are so sure you saw the boy from the barbecue in Venice yesterday. Or have you changed your mind?'

He released the lighter switch with a sharp click and the flame died.

Michael nodded approvingly. There had been enough dialogue. In the end words meant nothing and the image became all important. This small scene was the stuff of which great direction was made. The extinguished flame was an invitation to confess more potent than any verbalization could be. It seemed almost churlish to refuse it. How might it go?

Big close-up. Michael's eyes. In them the lighter flame is reflected. Suddenly it goes out.

Medium shot. The two men face each other across the table.

Crane shot. From above, the square table with the chequered cloth looks like a chessboard. Suddenly Michael's hand flicks out and knocks over his cup like a chess player conceding a game. The coffee stain spreads.

Medium shot. Contarini rises. He is wearing white tie and tails. From out of shot someone throws a top-hat and a cane which he catches expertly. The title number from *Top Hat* is played. Contarini leaps on the table and starts dancing. He moves from table to table till he reaches Sarah, who is wearing a long flowing diaphonous white evening gown. He pulls her on to the table with him. They whirl madly round the room, ending up at one end, with the Truemans, the Lovelaces, Dunkerley, Aristide and Michael standing against a whitewashed wall at the other. Using his cane as a rifle and his heels to tap out shots, Contarini shoots them one by one till only Michael remains. Contarini shoots. For a moment it looks as if Michael is unharmed, then like Jerry the cartoon cat he fragments like a shattered statue and collapses to a heap of unrecognizable sherds.

Cut! Why can't I keep it straight? Michael asked himself angrily.

He stood up.

'I mustn't keep you from your work, Captain,' he said. 'You are going back to Rimini today, I believe you said.'

Contarini smiled, gracious in defeat.

'Perhaps,' he said. 'We would still like to look at the clothes you were wearing, Mr Masson. My men are searching hard for this French boy, Aristide. Should he return the clothes to you here at the hotel, you will of course inform me?'

'Of course.'

'Then good day.'

With a wave at the spectator table, Contarini left. Michael made a business of drinking the last dregs of his coffee till his hand stopped shaking. It had been frightening, the certainty that he was about to be arrested. What had made Contarini draw back at the last minute? His failure to extract an admission of guilt? A recognition of the flimsiness of his case? Or just a reasonable doubt – if Italian law recognized such a thing.

Whatever the reason, for the moment he was free. But he had a feeling that unless the captain found someone else who looked a better bet than himself, Michael Masson's name was likely to be missing from the flight-list to Luton.

It was time for a bit of private detecting, and to start with he wanted to talk to these so-called holiday friends whose attitude to the truth was so cavalier. But before he could even draw back his upper lip preparatory to a Bogart lisp, the hotel manager entered.

'Please, is the Signor Trueman here?' he asked generally of the dining-room.

'No,' said Michael. 'He's gone out.'

'Where he go?' demanded the manager.

'I don't know. Why? Is something wrong?'

'Is his wife. Is very ill. I have call *il dottore*. Maybe she die, I think.'

If Wendy was going to die, it was clear she was going to do it before a full house. Sarah, who had been prevented only by pregnancy from spending a year in Central Africa as a volunteer hospital worker (this was while Michael was still in his social realism phase), had naturally rushed to Wendy's bedside, dislodging thence a maternal cleaning woman and the head waiter, whose eyes grew wild like Captain Ahab's every time the white whale of Wendy's bosom surfaced from the storm-tossed bedding.

'He's poisoned me, he's poisoned me; don't go, don't go!' she cried, clutching at the cleaner. 'Where's Michael? He understands. Oh, Michael!'

Michael, hovering in the corridor, entered at the sound of his name.

'I'm here,' he said.

'Oh good! Oh thank you! He's killed me, I said he would. Are Bob and Molly there?'

Bob and Molly were summoned, the manager appeared, the head waiter was joined at the open door by an appreciative claque of his underlings, and the doctor when he finally arrived found it almost impossible to get into the room.

Sarah had already diagnosed a high fever and the doctor confirmed this with his thermometer. He made some effort to have the room cleared, but the slightest vale-dictory movement on anyone's part brought such a spasm of protest from the sick woman that he abandoned the attempt, insisting only that the spectators withdrew from the immediate bedside.

'Tell him to look for poison,' Wendy instructed Sarah.

'I don't know the words,' confessed Sarah, whose three months' induction course had given her a grounding in Kikuyu but left her Italian pretty well untouched.

She turned to the manager.

'What is poison? How do you say poison?'

K

'Poison!' the manager screamed. 'Poison? No poison! Who say poison? Clean kitchen, everything fresh! My family eat, you eat, why not everyone poison?'

'I seem to have interrupted a misunderstanding.'

It was Dunkerley, wearing the usual grey gym-shoes and baggy slacks. Sarah was more pleased to see him than she would have thought possible.

'Oh, Sydney, would you translate? Wendy's ill, she wants to talk to the doctor.'

'Of course.'

Wendy's version of her illness was that she had woken in the night with severe stomach pains and had twice been sick in the bathroom. She had slept fitfully for a couple of hours till morning when she had awoken to find Wilf, fully dressed, looking down at her. He had told her she deserved what she got for making such a pig of herself with the vino the previous night and offered her a glass of water mixed with what he said was a stomach powder. She drank it. He left. Fifteen minutes later she felt very ill indeed. She had risen, been sick, and asked the maternal cleaner to summon help.

The doctor asked questions and talked at length to Dunkerley, while the manager kept up an unremitting stream of protest against the anticipated criticisms of his cuisine.

Finally Dunkerley addressed the English-speaking contingent.

'There is nothing to worry about, it seems. When I told the doctor about Mrs Trueman's unfortunate immersion in the canal yesterday, he felt this explained everything. She was foolish not to take medical advice immediately. He intends to give her an injection now, and this, coupled with some antibiotic medication to be taken orally, should see her fit and well in twenty-four hours.'

Everyone smiled and looked relieved except Wendy.

'Fools, fools!' she said. 'He's killing me, can't you see? He's killing me! Michael, you believe me, don't you?'

She seized his hand in a grip whose strength ill became a wronged and dying maiden.

'Yes, yes, of course I do. Of course I do,' he said.

'Well, tell that stupid sod!' she commanded, pointing dramatically at the doctor. 'I was a nurse before I got trapped. I know how thick these bastards can be! Butchers, butchers!'

The doctor needed no translation to recognize abuse and his patience snapped. Gesticulating angrily, he drove them from the room, all the time talking at such a speed that Dunkerley's meticulous and detailed translation continued for some moments after they had been shut out in the corridor.

'. . . silly fat English-er-lady; poisoned, she perhaps needs to be poisoned, get out, get out, this is not the Fenice theatre, uncivilized, they come to Venice, they know nothing, nothing, go, go, go . . .'

'That woman's hysterical,' said Bob.

'She sounded quite normal to me,' said Molly.

'Did she?' grunted her husband. 'Well, all I say is, anyone who goes around agreeing with what she says wants to be careful. That's all.'

'Meaning me?' said Michael.

'If the cap fits,' said Bob.

He turned away, but Michael, made brave by irritation, grasped his shoulder. Immediately the burly figure dipped and twisted, seized Michael's elbow in one hand, his wrist in the other and forced his arm up behind his back. He shrieked in pain and the grip was released, not, he realized when the tears left his eyes, on humanitarian grounds but as a result of a combined attack from Molly and Sarah. Molly was using a classical left hook to the shoulder while Sarah was concentrating on hacking his kneecap off with the side of her foot. She looked surprisingly expert and Michael wondered if she had fitted a Kung Fu class into her extra-mural courses.

'Ladies, ladies!' protested Dunkerley. 'You are overlooked!'

The head waiter and his minions had paused in their descent of the stairs and were grouping for yet another performance by this talented English company.

The two women halted their attack. Sarah turned to

Michael and put her arm comfortingly round his shoulders.

'Are you all right?' she asked.

'I think so,' he said. 'Though I may never play at Wimbledon again. Christalmighty, I never knew what they meant by police brutality till now.'

'Police brutality?'

'Yes,' he said with some satisfaction. 'He, that thug there, is a policeman.'

Sarah and Dunkerley looked pleasingly surprised.

'That's why he's so coy about talking about his work,' continued Michael viciously. 'A bit ashamed, perhaps, so there might still be hope, eh, Constable Lovelace? Or is it Sergeant?'

'Chief Inspector,' said Bob. 'No, I'm not ashamed. If I had a nothing-job like yours, I might be. I just like peace and quiet on holiday, away from the jokers and the ghouls, both.'

It sounded reasonable, Michael had to admit, but the pain in his arm had nothing to do with reason. Sarah obviously felt the same.

'Being a policeman gives you no right to attack people,' she said.

'I was defending myself,' Bob protested. 'Man grabs you from behind, you've got to be able to handle yourself.'

'I see. So every time your children jump on your back, you knock them down?'

'Don't be daft!'

'They're not old enough yet,' said Molly. 'Another few years, when shouting at them doesn't work, then he'll start knocking them down.'

'At least I'd have brought them on holiday with us,' rejoined Bob angrily. 'It was you who went on about needing a break by ourselves.'

'Yes, I did. I wanted to see if we could still talk to each other,' said Molly.

She turned away and went rapidly down the stairs. Bob took an uncertain step after her, but Sarah pushed him aside, saying, 'Oh, don't bother!'

Left by themselves, the three men hesitated either to

speak or to move, as though waiting for some call to action. Finally Michael broke the silence.

'What the hell are you two playing at?' he said.

'I don't quite follow,' said Dunkerley.

'Well, for a start, when I left you by the swimming pool that night after we got back from Florence, I went straight back into the hotel. Contarini says you told him you didn't notice which direction I took. You must be blind!'

'Not blind, old chap. It's merely that I was extremely fatigued that night. My eyes closed the minute I lay down. I'm sorry, but I didn't think it was important. Look here, if you like, I'll have another word with the man, tell him I recollect now that you went straight back inside. Would that help?'

'Huh!' snorted Bob. 'It'll help you straight into an Italian gaol.'

'You'd like that,' said Michael. 'You'd like to see us all inside, I dare say. After all it's your job. Is that why you lied about Florence?'

'What?'

'I told Contarini what happened in Signora Beatrice's place. He said he got a different version from you, one which said you and me did no screwing. Convenient, that. It nicely protects your lily-white constabulary reputation and at the same time drops me in the crap.'

'What the hell are you on about?' demanded Bob.

'All that stupid damn jealousy. Fortunately it's not just your word. Dunkerley was there too and he won't be ashamed of the truth.'

'What? Me? Certainly not,' said Dunkerley. 'Anything you say, Michael.'

Bob was beginning to turn red with anger, presumably at the reference to his jealousy, and while Michael felt very capable of dealing with him verbally, he wasn't ready for another physical confrontation. He could recollect many cinematic struggles in which the apparently weaker contender by either skill or cunning overcame his opponent. Spencer Tracy versus Ernest Borgnine in *Bad Day at Black Rock* for instance. But all he had in common with Tracy at the moment was that he only had the use of one arm, and any attempt to karate chop Bob would probably quickly lose him the use of the other.

'You're just a civilian here, Chief Inspector,' he said. 'If you want to get back safely to directing traffic, you won't forget it.'

He set off downstairs at the greatest speed he could manage this side of flight and did not stop walking till, led perhaps by some deep-buried instinct for sanctuary, he found himself in the golden darkness of St Mark's.

Here he sat, considering lighting problems, till a party of Germans surrounded him and their incomprehensible jabber disrupted his musings. Suddenly he wanted air and light. He knew where to get them. A short walk across the square, a short wait in a queue, a short journey in a lift, and he was two hundred feet above the city in the belfry of the campanile. Below in the square the tourists strolled around like pigeons and the pigeons ran like ants. It was a tremendous vantage point. Up here a man with a camera could command all approaches to the heart of the city. Venice, he decided, was a film set with the intriguing extra of having had backs built on to all the frontages during the centuries spent waiting for the movie camera.

Suddenly he pressed close to the wire mesh which prevented accidental spillage of human flesh to the distant ground, though it did not rise high enough to contain a nimble suicide.

Below, just entering the piazzetta between the columns of St Mark and St Theodore, was a figure in a red shirt, no more than a colourful doll among a myriad of others from up here. But it seemed to Michael that something about his movement made him stand out. It was absurd. This distance, this elevation – how could any kind of identification be made?

He followed him as far as he could, lost him for a while as he passed close to the campanile and the wire made it impossible to peer straight down, then picked him up once more and with growing excitement saw him sit at a table outside Florian's. A waiter approached. An order was given. He would be there for some time. No one paid Florian's prices and downed his drink in one! Impatiently Michael turned and waited for the lift to make its rattling ascent.

'Don't you worry about Bob when he's at work?' asked Sarah.

'I used to a bit. Not now. I just don't think about him. Why? Do you worry about Michael?'

'No,' said Sarah in surprise. 'Why should I?'

'Why not?'

'Well, it's not the same. There aren't the same dangers.'

'No, but there must be others. All those students. He's quite attractive when he's not flashing his boyish smile.'

Sarah was taken aback by this frankness.

'I don't know if I like that,' she said.

'What I said? Or just saying it?'

'Just saying it, I think.'

'Well,' said Molly, 'you've been very ready with lots of personal comment on my life and relationships, for which I'm very grateful, believe me. And any moment now we're going to get on to the fascist police state, I'm willing to bet. So can't I be honest and open too?'

Sarah thought about it for a moment.

'Yes, of course you can,' she said. 'But it's not quite as nice as me being open and honest, I must admit. What do you mean? He hasn't tried anything with you, has he?'

'Oh no! Though there was a moment at dinner last night when he gave me a funny look. No, I just wondered about him, that's all. I was dead frightened of him at first, but that just lasted a few days. That's one of the things that makes me feel I'd like to try something new, something that takes a bit of brain. All the bright people I meet are really formidable at first, then after a while, well, they just aren't any more. They're still brighter than me, but they're not *different*, if you understand. Most of Bob's mates just bore me stiff!'

'Did I frighten you too?' asked Sarah.

'You? Oh no. I mean, I've met lots like you.'

Sarah liked this even less. To work for the betterment

of the masses shouldn't necessarily mean being submerged in them.

'Michael's a bit weird though, isn't he?' continued Molly thoughtfully. 'You don't think he *could* have had anything to do with that Rimini business, do you?'

Now Sarah grew really indignant.

'Look here,' she said. 'I've got to draw a line somewhere!'

'That's all right. I just wondered where you'd draw it. All right. Suppose you found out he *had* done something like that, how would you react?'

Sarah nibbled a bit of chicken while she thought this one out. The two women were having lunch together. Michael and Wilf had not returned, Bob had announced he wasn't hungry, and Wendy was still in bed though much improved.

Molly, having tasted the once forbidden joys of verbalization, grew impatient of the silence.

'That's the only thing about Bob's work I was ever really interested in,' she resumed. 'Whenever they got a rapist, or a child molester, or a killer, I'd ask about his wife. It used to drive him wild. I should have been asking about the clever part he'd played in sorting out the case, I suppose. But he once said he reckoned in ninety per cent of the cases, they knew.'

'Knew about their husbands?'

'That's it. Not knew for certain, you understand, but well, they weren't surprised. Shattered, yes, but not surprised. Well, it makes sense, doesn't it? There's nothing Bob could do that would surprise me. Not even shatter me.'

She glanced at her watch.

'This service is pretty lousy, isn't it? I've got to dash. I'm sorry, no time for pudding. Anyway, it'll keep me trim. You have mine. You're OK. You're one of the lucky ones, you'll stay nice and skinny for ever. Bye!'

Sarah watched her go with mixed feelings. She remembered that Michael had once told her her humanitarian instincts were like mother love, an excuse for possession. Like most of Michael's insights, it was pushed

over the bourne of that cynicism which is the common
refuge of the romantic sentimentalist. She had once
caught him sobbing his heart out at a television showing
of *Lassie Come Home* and she had had to take the children
by herself to see *Dumbo*. But it *was* a real insight for all that.
Places and people alike, she wanted the freehold of. If she
discovered a new restaurant or a new writer, she resented
the intrusion of others even at her own recommendation.
And lame dogs once over the stile and cured had a dis-
concerting habit of galloping away over the skyline.
Unlike Lassie, they rarely came home.

So goodbye Molly. The sight of her pummelling her
husband this morning had confirmed her emancipation.
No revolution was complete without an act of violence.
Poor Wendy now, what hope for her? She was a victim,
on the surface so much more outspoken and experienced
than Molly, but really like a child terrorized by a brutal
step-father but more terrified still of the unknown world
outside her garret.

Sarah liked the image, though her social psychology
course had warned her of the dangers of developing
analogies too far. Wilf was a husband, not a step-father.
Wendy's garret was luxuriously appointed and the great
unknown must surely be peopled with friends and
relations, not to mention the social agencies and the law.

Nevertheless she was lying alone and unwell at this very
moment in a hotel bedroom in a foreign land. She was in a
very real sense a refugee, close kin to those tens of thousands
who almost daily, it seemed, were to be seen bearing their
few possessions and their frightened children along distant
dusty roads towards some inconceivable sanctuary.

Sarah finished her pudding, rose, helped herself to
coffee and went upstairs.

Wendy was sitting up in bed looking pale and petulant.
A tray with untouched food on it rested in front of her.
She was smoking and flicking the ash with savage satis-
faction on to the chicken and chips.

'Where is the bastard?' she demanded. 'That's what
I'd like to know. Where the hell is he?'

'How are you feeling?' asked Sarah.

'Lousy. But I'm getting up. Take this away, will you?'

Sarah removed the tray to prevent its being cast to the ground.

'Is that wise?' she asked.

'What's wise? I'll be better up. I'm too easy a target lying around like this.'

She staggered as she put her weight on her feet and Sarah anxiously offered her support.

'No. I'm all right. I need a swill down, and I'll be fine.'

She struggled out of her nightdress and to Sarah's distress began to wash herself stark naked, rubbing a cloth soaked in cold water under her arms and over the whole of her torso.

'That's better, that's better. Christ, those bruises haven't gone yet.'

Unwillingly Sarah let her attention be drawn to an area of discoloration on the rib-cage, then her inhibitions faded as she realized what it signified.

'Is that where he hit you? The swine! Oh, you must do something about this, Wendy.'

Wendy shrugged and lit another cigarette.

'You tell me what and I'll do it.'

'See your solicitor,' advised Sarah. 'Divorce him.'

Wendy mulled over the thought for a while, absently patting herself dry with a hand towel.

'All right,' she said finally. 'Thanks. I will.'

Sarah was surprised. She also felt that in some undesirable way responsibility had been transferred to herself.

'Make sure that's what you want,' she urged.

'Oh, there's no doubt of that. Things can't go on like this. I'd leave the bastard here and now, only we're on the same passport.'

There was a knock at the door.

'Come in,' called Wendy, but Sarah with a much deeper ingrained sense of the proprieties dashed to the door and opened it a crack.

It was Dunkerley.

'Oh, good day, Mrs Masson, Sarah. I was just wondering how our invalid was faring.'

'Who is it?' asked Wendy.

'It's Mr Dunkerley,' said Sarah, keeping a firm pressure against the door.

'Oh. His little friend's not with him, come to finish me off, is he?'

Wendy rose as if to confront her visitor. If she was as insensitive to the ocular stimulus of her body with Wilf, perhaps his evident frustration was in part understandable.

'You get dressed, Wendy,' said Sarah firmly. 'Then come downstairs to the bar. A drink and a breath of fresh air will do you good.'

She slid her thin frame round the door and joined Dunkerley on the landing.

'What did she say?' asked the fat man.

'Oh nothing. She's getting changed. You can buy me a drink.'

'Something about Aristide, wasn't it? She's not still making that absurd allegation, is she?'

Something unconvincing in Dunkerley's tone struck Sarah and she found herself saying, 'Michael told me that Wilf had made you an offer to do away with Wendy, so what's so absurd about it?'

They descended the stairs in silence, Sarah at the same time regretful and excited at what she had said.

In the bar, Dunkerley ordered a Punt e Mes for himself and out of curiosity she tried it also. It was rather disappointing, nothing near as exotic as she had imagined.

'I told Michael in confidence,' said Dunkerley reproachfully. 'I'm very disappointed in him.'

'Confidences automatically include wives,' defended Sarah.

'Yes, I suppose so,' he answered doubtfully.

'What he didn't tell me was if you accepted the offer.'

'Me?' said Dunkerley. Then repeated in tones of greater amusement. 'Me? *Me*? My dear lady, what do you take me for?'

'You're a professional killer, aren't you? A mercenary. Or don't black men count?'

Her indignation swept over Dunkerley but left him untouched.

'Black men, white men. I'm like anyone else, my dear Sarah. I'd possibly kill for revenge, jealousy, anger, and colour would make no difference. But not for money. Oh no. I have no stomach for it.'

'But you said . . .'

He shrugged.

'When you're hoping for a free drink, perhaps a free ride, you say whatever you imagine people would like to hear. It is true that once in a moment of extreme deprivation both of lucre and good sense, I did sign on as an African mercenary some years ago. I realized very quickly it was not, as they say, my scene. I had the good sense to confess and after some initial unpleasantness – I had, after all, concocted a fairly distinguished military record in order to get the job – I was put into the cookhouse till such time as I was able to leave the country. I am a cook of some ability, I might add, and they were in the end most reluctant to see me go. But I insisted. Your average black revolutionary has no means of distinguishing non-combatant practitioners of *haute cuisine* from the common soldiery.'

He emptied his glass.

'Another drink?'

'Oh please, let me.'

'I'm glad you said that. Funds are low. But I thought you might offer. I have made you feel a little guilty, I think. You are unusual in this, my dear Sarah. Normally my reputation as a killer is what impresses the ladies. They want details. It can be very exciting. But the way to your heart is through your conscience, I see.'

Sarah paid for the drinks thoughtfully.

'I've been thinking about what you told me the other night. About Aristide. Why did you bother to tell me?'

'It seemed, how shall I put it, only fair.'

'You were afraid my ego might be bruised?' said Sarah disbelievingly.

'In some degree.'

'But it was more for your own benefit, I'm sure,' went on Sarah.

'My dear, don't hesitate to say what must be obvious. I

am in love with Aristide, yes. We wander across Europe
like outlaws through the greenwood, except that no one
much cares nowadays! Still it's a romantic concept.
Anyway, like outlaws, we must rob the rich to feed the
poor; that is, ourselves. When we saw how you had taken
to Aristide, it seemed too good an opportunity to miss.'

'Opportunity for what?' said Sarah.

'Well, you weren't worth robbing. Aristide checked
through your luggage and, honestly, there was nothing
worth the trouble of fencing. But doubtless you have some
money and the usual banker's apparatus for getting more.
Aristide felt able to manage a flirtation with some
expensive presents thrown in. He's done it before. Unfortunately you moved a little too fast for him, I'm afraid.'

Sarah flushed with shame and anger.

'You're being very frank, Mr Dunkerley, especially
for someone who's so concerned about my bruised ego.
Why *did* you come to see me yesterday? Not because you
were jealous surely?'

Dunkerley drank and smiled, then placed his empty
glass significantly on the bar.

'It may surprise you, dear Sarah, but even a broken-
down old queen like me doesn't much care to know that
his friend has been sexually assaulted. I didn't want a
repeat. Aristide is young, susceptible. I should hate him
to be led astray.'

'Is that why you quarrelled? About me?'

Dunkerley hesitated.

'No,' he said. 'No. That was another matter. But we
must not digress. I came to tell you last night that I had
discarded Plan A for getting money out of you, but before
I could produce Plan B that gorgeous policeman appeared.
May I have another drink?'

'That depends on how good Plan B is,' said Sarah,
feeling marvellously cool and controlled.

'Not very subtle, I fear. Pay up or I tell Michael about
your attempt on Aristide.'

'No, that isn't very subtle,' agreed Sarah. 'Especially
as Michael's already convinced we've been to bed
together.'

'Yes, that did strike me,' said Dunkerley. 'Still, I felt it worth a try. However, the events of yesterday and an interview I had late last night with Captain Contarini have persuaded me to scrap Plan B also and move on to Plan C. You see, I have a bad memory and poor powers of observation, so I am presently attempting to piece together all those fragments of time involving both your husband and myself in the past few days.'

Through the bar door Sarah saw Wendy appear. She felt uncertain whether to be relieved or not when she did not come into the bar but turned away towards the reception desk.

'Contarini is particularly interested in what really happened in Florence, and what Michael said and which direction he went in as he left me by the swimming pool that night. He would also, I'm sure, be interested in extracts from the conversations I had with Michael yesterday afternoon. And finally he's very keen to find Aristide to recover Michael's shirt. Whether you wish this or do not wish it is best known to yourselves. But an arrangement could be made.'

'You do know where Aristide's living then?'

Dunkerley shrugged.

'I will find out and quicker than the police. Venice is a village.'

'I can't imagine what leverage you imagine you can apply with your threats of lies and evasions,' said Sarah. 'But what do you hope to get from us?'

'Charity,' said Dunkerley. 'That is all. A resettlement grant. I am keen to see the white cliffs again. I grow old. We'll go no more a-roving. I should like to take Ari to England with me. Our separation is temporary, a mere tiff. But funds are low. I appeal to you.'

'You revolt me,' said Sarah. 'Why approach me? Why not Michael.'

'Men can become violent before they have time to think.'

'And you don't mind being violent with women,' sneered Sarah. 'Like slitting prostitute's faces.'

'What?' said Dunkerley, looking surprised. 'Who said
. . .? Ah! Aristide. He told you that was me? Well, well.
Of course he would. How observant of him. Another
woman he might have told the truth to, but you, you
could only be titillated by violence at a stage removed.
Like I said, that conscience of yours!'

'What are you saying?' demanded Sarah. 'That it was
Aristide . . .?'

'Of course! Just look at us! Listen, Sarah, whatever
else happens in this, don't let Michael go near Aristide.
He is a dangerous man, believe me. In all kinds of ways.'

He spoke with an urgency which struck Sarah as
genuine. Suddenly something which had been puzzling
her made sense.

'That's why you fell out!' she said. 'Not because of me
but because he'd been in the canal with Wendy. *You*
thought what she thought, that he was trying to drown
her!'

'Come, come!' said Dunkerley. 'Such fantasies.'

'No, it fits. You're all right for a bit of extortion, but
you don't care for killing people. So Wilf picked the
wrong one with you, even if he did mean it. But when
you told Ari, just for a laugh, he didn't find it funny,
simply a straightforward business deal. So, a quarrel.
Did he promise to be good? And next thing, you meet him
in Michael's clothes and find he's been swimming with
Wendy!'

'What an imagination you have,' mocked Dunkerley.
'Let us not forget where we were, however. Have you
made up your mind?'

'I've made up *my* mind,' said Wendy firmly, sliding on
to a stool and rapping on the bar. Dunkerley looked at
her with distaste, Sarah with much relief.

'Let me buy you a drink,' she said brightly. 'Mr
Dunkerley's just going.'

Dunkerley smiled and rose.

'I look forward to another talk soon about the old
country,' he said. 'Good day to you both.'

'Fat creep,' said Wendy. 'How do I go about getting a

divorce? You know about these things. You're a practical woman.'

Sarah should have been distraught at Dunkerley's threats, but instead she found herself almost completely unmoved. Perhaps she *was* a practical woman, too practical at any rate to want to be drawn any further at this juncture into Wendy's marital problems.

'You're a practical woman yourself,' she said. 'Being a nurse is practical.'

It was a pretty soft attempt at blackmail, really, she assured herself. There was no substance there. Dunkerley had tried to play it very cool as if modelling himself on that big fat man who played villains opposite Humphrey Bogart in those tedious thrillers Michael raved about . . . Sydney Greenstreet; they even shared a name! But beneath it all there had been an uneasiness.

'No. Nurses aren't practical,' contradicted Wendy. 'Nurses are terrified of the people who boss them. The only people nurses can deal with are poor sods on their backs full of pain and pills.'

This was heart-baring with a vengeance! Normally Sarah would have been delighted to peer and probe at the pulsating mass of muscle and membrane, but there were other diagnoses and prognoses to be made much nearer home.

'Let's talk about it later,' she said brightly. 'Oh Jesus Christ!'

Blasphemous oaths did not come easily to her lips despite her teenage recognition of the hypocrisies and abuses of the Church, but the apparition at the bar door of Michael, his clothes dusty and torn, his face bruised with one eye grossly swollen, merited a cosmic reaction.

The barman took one look and went to fetch the manager, who covered his eyes when he saw Michael and broke into a long *recitativo* whose words were undistinguishable but whose meaning was unmistakable.

Wendy, confronted by a helpless man, demonstrated the truth of the second part of her nursing analysis by springing into rapid action and while she sought out and dressed Michael's wounds, Sarah cradled his head in best dying-hero fashion and sought to discover what had happened.

'I don't know who did it. I was just strolling round the back streets somewhere near a fish market near the Rialto Bridge. There were a lot of people around at first, then I turned a couple of corners and found myself in a little dark alleyway. There was a large wooden door set in the wall and through a crack in it I could see greenery as though a garden lay beyond. I had a sense of gracious, luxurious civilized living going on behind that door, you know, as if the real culture of Venice still survived here, untouched by the tourist trappings. It was a sort of garden of the Finzi Continis. I really wanted to get inside, to somehow dolly up to the door, then dissolve the frame and pass through. You'd need a subtle lighting change, of course, a soft front light as if it had come through the door with you. But outside it's all one solid block of shadow with the sun-line only touching the wall some fifteen or twenty feet up.

'Anyway I stood by the door for some time. There was a cat there too, a black and grey cat sitting patiently regarding the door as if he belonged inside. I felt that perhaps someone would open it to let him in if I waited. He ignored me. I stooped to scratch his head and someone hit me, kicked me I think, so that I crashed head first against the door. I didn't fall through, but I was very dazed. Then I was punched on the head and face till I fell to the ground. I never saw who did it, not even a glimpse. All I recall as I lay there was that, as if attracted by my head banging against the woodwork, someone opened the door and the little cat who hadn't moved during all this commotion stepped inside. Then the door closed again. There *was* a different light in there. I glimpsed it for a moment.'

'Oh Michael,' said Sarah despairingly, knowing that Michael's script required no other reaction.

'Well, I think he'll survive. Let's get him upstairs,' said Wendy briskly. 'A couple of hours' rest and he'll be

L

fit for anything.'

Sarah took one arm, Wendy the other, and between them they helped Michael to the bedroom. Here Wendy set about removing his shirt and sandals with professiona ease and would have happily stripped him completely i Sarah had not prevented her.

'I think we can manage now,' she said. 'Thanks fo your help.'

'What? Oh, yes. I see. I got carried away. He'll be all right now. You know, I feel much better myself. I think I'll have a stroll and look at a sodding church o something.'

After her departure, Sarah completed the undressing and got Michael into bed.

'How on earth did you manage to get back?' she asked 'Didn't anyone help you?'

He grimaced.

'Not bloody likely. I got a few funny looks, that's all There's every race in the world in St Mark's Square, they say, but there can't be many Samaritans.'

'Who did it, Michael? Have you got no idea?'

'I told you. None at all.'

'Could it have been Bob? Or Aristide? Wilf even?'

'For God's sake, why? Probably just some local mugger.'

'Were you robbed? Did he take anything?'

'God knows. I haven't looked. You check if you like, I just want to close my eyes for a while.'

He turned his best cheek to the pillow. The swollen eye which remained uppermost took very little closing. Sarah switched off the light which the gloominess of the room rendered necessary even in the middle of the day and took Michael's clothes over to the window to examine the contents of his pockets. The window was side open to let in the air and she leaned out in search of coolness. Below her in the narrow *calle* someone moved. She glanced down.

It was Aristide.

He hadn't seen her, his attention seemed fixed on the junction of the narrow passageway with the sunlit street where the hotel's main entrance stood. Could he have followed Michael back here? Or was he perhaps waiting for herself to appear? She considered the possibility calmly. Today she seemed to be able to consider everything calmly. The only thing that disturbed her at all was the extent of her own calmness.

Aristide stiffened, like an animal who senses someone approaching. Through the sunlight at the end of the alley walked Wendy, like the goddess Diana glimpsed through the trees, then was gone. Aristide followed.

Or perhaps he didn't follow. Perhaps he had been on the point of moving off, anyway.

Sarah grabbed her handbag, recollected her money was running very short, dropped Michael's billfold into it, and quietly left the room.

As she ran down the stairs she felt the same excitement she had experienced six months earlier when investigating an alleged case of misuse of police authority in a drugs raid on a local pub much used by young people. Sarah had sat in the pub for three nights in a row, waiting to be raided. She was treated respectfully by the regulars but their distressing habit of referring to her as 'Ma' as much as the non-appearance of the fuzz had made her abandon the stake-out. But on that first night she had felt an almost sexual excitement and this came back now as she tracked Aristide on the short walk to St Mark's Square. Here, however, the chase fizzled out. When Wendy said she was going to 'look at a sodding church', she meant just that and having taken a seat at Quadri's she sat facing the basilica and disposing of a succession of drinks for the next hour and a half.

Aristide meanwhile had perched himself at the foot of one of the three great flag poles which soar in front of St Mark's, while Sarah hung around the main portal of the church itself. Here she was in the shade and camouflaged by the constant ebb and flow of tourists who took their sight-seeing more energetically than Wendy.

It was Aristide whose patience broke first, assuming of course that he *was* there in pursuit of Wendy and not just coincidentally. He stood up, his thin young face full of irritation, and slouched away across the square. Sarah followed. Her initial motivation for following had disappeared but, as jolly fox-hunting vice-presidents of the RSPCA have found for years, the chase is more important than the object of the chase.

It presented no problems. Aristide moved fairly slowly, his head bent forward, as though in deep thought. They crossed the Rialto Bridge passing stalls ablaze with huge green melons, yellow peaches, vein-hued aubergines, fiery tomatoes, smoke-white fungi, black and onyx grapes. That part of Sarah's schizophrenic housewifery which lusted for the fresh and the seasonal was warmed to ecstasy at the sight, and for a moment the other Consumer-Association-deep-freeze-best-buy part dwindled almost to oblivion. She might have lost Aristide here had he not paused, then resumed his progress past a mound of peaches with a motion unidentifiably familiar till she recalled his shoplifting demonstration on the beach at Rimini.

The stallkeeper looked after him suspiciously but decided that pursuit and accusation were not worth the effort. After a while Aristide, sucking his stolen peach, began to bear left, leaving the market area behind him, including the fish market which Sarah recalled Michael mentioning in his account of the assault. Could this be significant? She doubted it. She had other theories.

They crossed a campo dominated by the inevitable church, turned right, crossed a canal, followed it for a while, then Aristide plunged into a passageway narrow even by Venetian standards and Sarah reached the end of it just in time to see him turning into a doorway.

The time had come to ask herself just what she was doing. The answer was *nothing* if it ended here. She entered the passageway and, observed only by the unblinking and totally indifferent eyes of a small child sitting on the threshold, she passed through the doorway.

Inside it was dark enough to make her halt till her sight had adjusted. The air was very warm and rich with the smells of cooking and living. A staircase rose straight ahead but to her right was a passage from which led three doors. She approached the first stealthily and listened. She heard nothing and she passed on. As she applied her ear close to the next, the third door opened.

'*Nom de dieu! Qu'est-ce que vous foutez là?*' cried an angry voice. And a hand seized her by the elbow and dragged her roughly into the room.

IV

Michael had slept for a while, and when he awoke, Contarini was sitting at his bedside reading an Italian film magazine.

'I thought you'd gone back to Rimini,' said Michael.

'Almost. What's your opinion of Kelly?'

'Grace?'

'Gene. Too much muscle, too much energy, I think. Yet a fine inventive mind. He is himself, always. But I prefer Astaire.'

'Why haven't you gone back to Rimini?'

Contarini leaned close and regarded him sadly.

'I am not my own master, Signor Masson. Which of us is? We all must do what our natures dictate to us. To do less is a betrayal of whatever has created us.'

'Do stop talking balls, Contarini, and pass me a cigarette.'

Contarini complied and lit it with a match.

'Forgive me. I had forgotten that England is the birthplace of the anti-intellectual tradition, particularly your universities and colleges. I should have said simply that my superiors have ordered me to remain in Venice for the present. I am sorry to learn of your misfortune.'

'It wasn't much. Just some thug. You meet them everywhere.'

'Of course. Good. I am glad you do not hold it against the administration of my city. But the English have always loved Venice. And we Venetians love the English best of all our visitors. I spend a holiday once, sometimes twice a year in England. I lived in London for three years as a teenager, did I tell you that? I have English Language at 'O' Level.'

'Which is more than some of my compatriots have at any level,' observed Michael. 'I should like to get up now.'

'Please do. You find your work interesting?'

'Yes,' said Michael, flinging back the coverlet. He felt disadvantaged lying in bed while Contarini talked to him, but obviously the policeman was not going to leave to let him dress. He winced as he stood up.

'Good. Good. A man should be interested in his work. Tell me, Mr Masson, with your great love of the Italian cinema, why have you not learned our language?'

'I know enough to get by. I study scripts. I know when the sub-titles are lying. But I have no real gift for languages, unlike yourself.'

'Thank you. The post-war films interest me greatly. *Roma, città aperta, Ladri di biciclette, La terra trema,* the whole period of social realism. Fellini's *I Vitelloni* . . .'

'Hardly that.'

'What?'

'Neo-realism is important, of course, and produced its masterpieces. I do not think *I Vitelloni* is one of them. A masterpiece, yes, but not a neo-realistic one.'

'No? It is so many years, but if I recall right, it is about a gang of middle-class layabouts, not young, not criminals, but with no – what is the word? – focus for living. This is sociological observation, yes?'

'If you say so,' said Michael, pulling on his trousers. He distrusted this chatty policeman. The days when he had felt that the cops were one of the great obstacles to civilized progress were long past, but he felt a sudden pang of nostalgia for the thick, monosyllabic bobbies of his youth. *All right, all right, come along, come along, move on, move on.* Bob the bobbie! Of course. He should have recognized him immediately. Perhaps they had met on the road to Aldermaston or in Trafalgar Square.

'You were arrested twice, for obstructing the police and using abusive language. The first time, in 1959 you refused to pay a fine and spent a week in jail. The second time, in 1961, you paid your fine. Nothing since. Either you have reformed, Mr Masson, or you have become cleverer.'

Contarini laughed as he spoke and for a second Michael missed the enormity of what he had just heard, so that when it did strike home, his indignation must have had a false ring, like a mis-timed line in a play.

'You've been checking up on me! For God's sake, what kind of world do we live in?'

'A world of records, computers, and international co-operation,' answered Contarini promptly. 'Surely a better world than one of ignorance, rumour and distrust? Do not be distressed, Mr Masson. It's just routine, as my English colleagues say. Anyone I meet on a case, I take what details I can and ask our records office to fill in the background if there is one. With foreigners it is more difficult, but I have many British contacts and there is of course Interpol, though that is only for big fish.'

'Which we aren't?'

'Oh no. Very small. Mrs Trueman, nothing known; Mrs Lovelace, nothing known; Chief Inspector Lovelace, nothing (naturally!) known; Mr Trueman, some pecca-dilloes involving your driving laws. And then we come to Mrs Masson. I was surprised. A long record, continuing many years after your own criminal career seems to have ended. Attempted assault on the American ambassador, hurling bags of flour at a South African Rugby Football team, illegal occupation of an empty house belonging to your local council; the list is extensive, though she too seems to have reached years of discretion. At least, nothing has happened for almost a year.'

'Perhaps she's plotting the big one,' observed Michael. 'A pigeon-kidnapping from St Mark's Square, to be offered in exchange for five hundred student agitators.'

He finished dressing, combed his hair and opened the bedroom door. Contarini did not move.

'You have moved right, I think, Mr Masson. Interesting, that. Or perhaps I speak too politically. Perhaps merely after a youth of activity and promise, you have at last become one of the *vitelloni*?'

'We all find our level, Captain,' said Michael. 'Even if it's English 'O' level. I'm going downstairs now.'

'I shall accompany you. By the way, I ran a check on Mr Dunkerley too, and his friend who borrowed your clothes.'

'Oh yes?'

'Mr Dunkerley is without doubt one of the *vitelloni*. A

drifter, a wastrel, some minor thefts, shoplifting, a stolen hen, that kind of thing. And soliciting.'

'Soliciting?'

'Yes. Men, of course. A pathetic character.'

'You surprise me. I thought he was a soldier of fortune, a mercenary?'

'Hardly. His compulsory military service was ended abruptly when he started sending the Regimental Sergeant Major flowers. His companion we still have not traced. But we have discovered things about him. His full name is Roussel, Aristide Roussel, and he is a much nastier piece of cake. No, I am sorry, piece of work. Theft also, but violence too. He slashed a woman's face in Marseilles and was suspected in connection with a fatal stabbing in Nice only last year.'

'Why are you telling me this?' asked Michael, halting at the foot of the stairs and peering into the public rooms. 'Surely it's confidential?'

Contarini took his arm.

'It is my job to protect as well as pursue, Mr Masson. These men have become associated with you. Beware of them. The police cannot watch over you night and day.'

'Why should they want to?' asked Michael.

'You are the one,' intoned Contarini.

'What?'

'Only you beneath the stars and under the sun. Night and day – you remember? Fred and Ginger. What a number! There's a hungry yearning burning . . . how does it go?'

'They don't write them like that any more,' said Michael. 'Well, if there's nothing else . . .'

'If you seek your friends, none are here, I'm afraid. I have looked already. But why should they be here? There is beauty enough for a lifetime here in this city, and you have so few days.'

'Is Aristide queer too?' asked Michael.

'It seems likely. Why, does it matter? Ah, you are thinking of your wife!'

God, which of this blabber-mouthed lot have you been

talking to now? wondered Michael.

'Forget to be jealous,' urged Contarini. 'But do not let Mrs Masson be too close to this man.'

'All right, Captain. Whatever you say. But you know, you still haven't told me why you've come to see me again.'

Contarini looked surprised.

'No. It was not you I came to see. Naturally when I heard of your accident, I went upstairs to offer my condolences. That is all. I shall return later. Good day.'

He left quickly, acknowledging the salute of the policeman by the exit with an elegant wave which was pure Max Linder. Michael watched him go, then went in search of some coffee to counter the dull ache which was the pip in a slice of darkness at the back of his skull.

As he drank it he thought a little about Contarini but found, rather to his pleasure, that he was if anything a little bored by the man. There was something very obvious even about his subtleties.

His best theory at the moment is that I killed that poor sod on the beach and he'll go along with this till something better crops up, thought Michael. Tracing me through the lighter seems such a master-stroke that he doesn't dare go back to Rimini with his tail between his legs. I wouldn't put it past him to manufacture some extra evidence, but I'm not sure he's bright enough. Interpol indeed! God! he's spent some money finding out I'm a backsliding leftie. He should have just asked Sarah.

Who, he recalled with a shock, may have been doing some evidence-planting too. That bell in the bed! But like so many of the good causes she chose to support, Aristide had turned out to be a ringer. Which, when you came to think about it, was the right word. *Do not let Mrs Masson get too close to him*, Contarini had said. Well, that shouldn't be difficult!

But why the deception? Was it aimed at him or at herself?

He felt much better suddenly. It was all this thinking. A stroll in the air, perhaps a glance at the Doge's Palace would set him up nicely. But no young men in red shirts.

Oh no. Sarah was not the only one who could pick losers.

If that was adultery you can keep it, thought Sarah. But it hadn't really been adultery; more like a demonstration. Aristide had assumed, and she could hardly blame him, that she had come to see him with the same intentions she had made so clear on their last encounter. The formula she had chosen to reassure him – *Sydney explained everything* – had for some reason proved to be the trigger of a desperate and at times almost despairing assault which fell short of rape only because her struggles were moderated by the feeling that he had it coming to him. Which was a great deal more than she felt about herself.

The room was basic, containing a bed, a rickety table, a hard chair, and managing to be overcrowded even with these. Through a half-open door opposite the main entrance, Sarah could see what looked like a cupboard converted into a kitchenette with a sink and a small stove. Aristide rose now, went through this door, stood close to the sink and began using it as a bidet. Sarah looked the other way. This surely beat even Avril-with-the-long-juddering-cry's story of the JP with the riding crop who wanted to be beaten in the back of a Mini.

'Are you trying to murder Wendy?' she asked, almost thinking aloud.

'Who say that?' he demanded so angrily that she turned to look at him. He stood in the kitchen doorway drying himself with what she hoped was not a tea-towel.

'No one,' she said, suddenly frightened. 'I just thought of it.'

'Dunkerley? He say it? Yes!' he nodded grimly. 'He say it.'

'No, no. Really. He came to see me. He wanted money so that you and he could go away together to England.'

'England! I never go to England! English are shit. You also. Go now, finish now, fuck off!'

He was very angry and looked capable of driving her half naked into the street.

'I'll go when I'm ready,' retorted Sarah boldly. She

was not after all a ravished virgin to be abandoned callously by her assailant; she was a mature adulteress who had made most of the running.

She got off the bed, gathered up her clothes and pushed past Aristide into the kitchen. If this was the only place to clean up, then it was hers by right of . . . she had to dismiss age and sex, and settled finally for force, shoulder-ing the young man (whose rage had moderated to bewilderment) into the living-room and slamming the door on his puzzled face.

She held the door shut until certain there was going to be no immediate pursuit, then applied herself to the business of repairs. A meticulous examination of herself with her compact mirror revealed no tell-tale scars of the kind Michael's encounter had produced. Using her handkerchief as a towel, she cleaned herself as best she could and began to dress, discovering to her dismay that her sun-top had come apart at the seams in the mêlée. Fortunately in her bag was the portable repair kit which was part of her day-to-day survival pack and she quickly threaded a needle and began sewing. She had just finished when she heard voices in the room outside.

Even though the language was French and even though to start with the interchange was at a fairly quiet level, she had no doubt that the new arrival was Dunkerley and that the two men were quarrelling.

Quickly she slipped on her sun-top and combed her hair. If she had to be discovered here, at least it wouldn't be with any sign of her recent activities on open display. She looked remarkably well, she thought, looking at herself in her mirror.

Outside the row had escalated and both men were now shouting. Lovers' quarrels transcended barriers of sex and nationality, she thought gloomily. Not much else did. At least with two men, they wouldn't start throwing things at each other.

There was a tremendous crash and the kitchen door shook as something splintered against the woodwork. Voices stopped and were replaced by a breathless grunting and the slither of feet, then came the sound of a blow, an open-handed slap she guessed, followed immediately by a much more solid punch and a gasp of pain.

She was suddenly keen to see the fight, despite being a member of the British anti-boxing lobby, and opened the door a crack. Her money, had she approved of gambling, would have been firmly on the younger and fitter man, but she saw at a glance she was wrong. Dunkerley may have been unsuited to blowing holes in black men in the jungle, but in a bar-room brawl situation he clearly knew his stuff. He was in the act of bringing his forehead sharply against Aristide's nose, at the same time kneeing him in the crotch. Perhaps the youth's nudity disadvantaged him, for the slasher of prostitutes looked out of his class here.

'You'll come to your senses,' Dunkerley opined as he performed this operation, speaking in English as no doubt he felt Aristide wouldn't much mind at the moment. 'Oh yes, you'll see. You'll come to your senses.'

Nodding vigorously to emphasize his belief, a gesture contradicted by the tears streaming down his face, he thrust Aristide violently from him, turned and left the room, closing the door gently behind him.

Aristide did a couple of crouching waltz turns across the room towards the kitchen door and collapsed heavily against it, forcing it shut. Sarah waited a moment before trying to open the door again and for a while began to think she was stuck in there till either Aristide moved of his own volition or someone arrived to move him. Finally, by dint of flinging herself bodily against the door, she managed to force it open sufficiently to squeeze through.

Aristide lay on the floor facing upwards, his thin body stretched out as though on an invisible rack and his lips drawn back in an agonized parody of his toothy smile. Blood was oozing from beneath him with a rapidity which Sarah would not have believed possible. In theory she should have been sick. She had little stomach for nastiness of this kind; drawing a chicken was a task she hated. But now she felt quite detached and was able to work out what had happened. Dunkerley's blows hadn't been enough to produce this kind of haemorrhage. The old wooden chair must have been the source of the mighty crash against the kitchen door. Only the seat had remained undamaged and this had fallen to the floor with one splintered leg pointing up at the ceiling.

Aristide had collapsed on to it and was now impaled.

Sarah looked round the squalid room and shuddered. Loveless sex, brutal violence. She thought of the thousands of women in rooms such as this whose daily expectations rose no higher. But no tears formed. Instead she felt a pitying superiority. Life for a woman was a series of male traps, but their great weakness was that they were designed to take you alive. The only efficient trap is one which kills as it catches. A woman of wit and intellect could gnaw, trick or bribe her way out of any other.

Aristide twitched and faintly groaned. *You'll come to your senses*, Dunkerley had promised. Perhaps he had an old-fashioned belief in the moral efficacy of physical chastisement. At last she felt some emotion. Poor Dunkerley.

The Doge's Palace was a great disappointment to Michael. The courtyard was superb but inside he was depressed by a series of gloomy chambers whose walls and ceilings were spread with a chauvinist jam of scenes from Venetian history. By the time he reached the Grand Council Chamber where this Venetian egocentricity aspired at last to something like sublimity, he had been over-faced and took refuge in a window-niche which gave him a view out over a hot desert of red tiles.

'Find what you sought for, old man?'

He turned to be met by a breath like a distiller's blessing.

'I was rather disappointed,' he said, turning aside his head.

'I feared you might be,' said Dunkerley. 'You should have accepted my assistance. The professional nose.'

It might have been 'the professional knows', but his forefinger touched the edge of his right nostril as he spoke, which Michael took as a useful visual aid.

'And what would you have advised?' enquired Michael.

To his surprise and horror, tears suddenly sparkled in Dunkerley's eyes.

'Nothing, nothing. All that's done with now.'

He glanced around furtively, then produced a bottle of grappa from inside his shirt.

'Snort?' he said, proffering it.

'No, thanks.'

Dunkerley disposed of a huge mouthful.

'Ah,' he said, 'that brings the roses to a maiden's cheeks,' apparently oblivious of the line of moisture already running down his own.

'What are you doing here?' demanded Michael.

'Resting. Meditating. I like this room. Do you know it was sometimes used as a banqueting hall? Thousands of guests. Happy days. Happy days. How soon they pass. Now what's it good for? A roller-skating rink. The way of the world. Snort?'

'No, thanks,' repeated Michael. 'Has something happened, Sydney? Are you in trouble?'

'No trouble at all. What can trouble men like us, Michael? Only women, eh? They're always a trouble, always have been. That Sarah of yours. There's a dangerous woman. But you'll know that. I'm just a simple soul. Ask little from life. Don't get bloody much either, but that's the way of it. All that matters is a friend, a bit of comfort. You'll know that too. But there's no way. I'm fifty, would you believe that? Never felt I belonged to these times. No. Fifty was once a real age. Now it's . . . You're right to compromise, Michael my friend. The only way. I see it now. Oh Jesus. Snort?'

'What's up?' asked Michael, curiously moved. 'Have you and Aristide quarrelled?'

'Aristide? What's Aristide to you? You and your bloody wife! Had to teach him a lesson. Had to show him who's . . . oh Christ!'

Michael became aware that an official-looking man was scrutinizing them carefully and he stepped back from the window preparatory to abandoning Dunkerley. But as he did so, the official approached the fat man in mid-snort and spoke to him in tones so redolent of contumely that no interpretation was necessary. In any case, Dunkerley's Italian was excellent and idiomatic as became apparent from the official's reaction to his reply. He seized Dunkerley by the arm and tried to drag the bottle from his hand. *Things that a wise man will leave alone, are a drunk with a bottle and a dog with a bone.* Wondering from what folk-memory he had dredged up that dreadful couplet, Michael unwillingly entered the fray. Why, he could not imagine. Dunkerley was drunk and potentially disorderly; he was also a low-level con-man and, according to Contarini, a liar and a thief. Perhaps, thought Michael, us *vitelloni* have got to stick together.

Prising the two men apart, he used the old peacetime method of bringing awkward foreigners to heel and shouted angrily at the official in his best upper-class accent.

To his surprise it seemed to work. The man stepped back and though he continued to talk like a runaway train, a note of explanation had crept into his voice.

'Enough!' said Michael sternly holding up his right hand, palm outwards. 'We shall leave.'

Seizing Dunkerley's bottle before it shattered on the marble floor, he began tugging and pushing the fat Englishman towards the exit. Here they paused while Dunkerley clasped his right upper arm with his left hand, bent his arm and thrust his clenched fist into the air at the same time blowing a raspberry.

'You *did* see the film,' said Michael as he supported him down the stairs into the courtyard.

'What's that? You're a decent fellow. Welcome any time in Burnham Beeches. Yes. I mean it. Take me home. Your bloody wife can keep her rotten money. You and me understand . . .'

Here he pushed his hand into Michael's shirt in a gesture which might have been a caress or merely pursuit of his bottle. Michael thrust him away in revulsion and handed over the grappa.

'Try to pull yourself together, Dunkerley,' he commanded, unable to drop the ruling class persona so recently adopted. 'And don't come round to our hotel bothering people again. Understand?'

He began to walk away. Dunkerley overtook him after very few paces.

'Understand? Yes. I understand everything. Aristide, both of you. It's filthy, you hear me? Well, you be careful, that's all. You and your friends. I should have let him kill that bloody woman, but not me, not my idea, respectable bloody tourists, you and your bloody wives, filth, all of you!'

They were out in the piazza now and heads were turning, attracted by the noise even where the language was not understood. Michael increased his pace. Behind him the voice faded, dissolved, was left behind.

But he fancied he heard it all the way back to the hotel.

The tables remained together and by the end of dinner the tacit truce declared between the warring parties of the six-some had warmed into a positive armistice. Even Wendy seemed disposed to treat her husband (who had returned at last from whatever doubtless illicit pleasures had been occupying his day) as something more than arachnid, albeit still less than human. Wilf for his part was in vacant or in pensive mood and shot forth only one or two of those flashes of merriment, with which he was wont to set the table on a roar; Bob on the other hand spoke more than was usual for him, as if making a desperate effort to display his basic humanity; Molly said little but smiled and looked happy; and Sarah said less but smiled and looked sad, a combination which Michael referred to as her sorrows-of-the-world expression.

After dinner to his surprise Sarah proposed that they should all stroll to the piazza to listen to the music and to his greater surprise, the others agreed. As they walked along her hand slipped through his arm and she pressed close to him.

They heard the music before they reached the square. It was light, airy, and labyrinthine without being in the least sinister, like Hampton Court Maze on a sunny day with the hedges cut down to two feet six. It emanated from the *Banda Municipala* raised on a dais in the middle of the

M

piazza between Florian's and Quadri's. A large crowd had gathered round to watch the precise batoning of the elderly conductor but there were plenty of empty chairs outside the cafés.

'Like the bandstand at Bognor,' grinned Wilf. 'Will they know *The Maid of the Mountain* do you think?'

Michael sighed but did not feel angry. How could you feel angry with a man who, if Dunkerley were to be believed, put his money where his mouth was in such an important matter as uxoricide? The world's Wilfs were unacknowledged legislators of mankind.

They sat at Florian's and ordered drinks. It was a magic occasion. The air was warm and soft, the façade of St Mark's shone darkly, and along the columns of the arcaded Procuratie and the Napoleonic Wing ran a double row of lamps casting a festive glow over the dignified façades like Christmas candles in the branches of a living pine forest.

Now the music changed. After a bout of appreciative applause, the conductor drove his team into the richer pastures of Verdi's *Aïda*.

Suddenly Michael felt safe. Here, if anywhere, surely that ghastly world which others mistook for reality could not intrude. Here he and Sarah could be happy and innocent like Hugo and Josefin in Kjell Grede's film. He reached out and took Sarah's hand.

'Isn't this the life?' he murmured.

'Oh, it is, it is,' said a figure behind them which he had assumed to be a waiter keeping an eye open for defaulting customers.

'May I be permitted to join you?' And without staying for an answer Contarini pulled up a chair alongside them.

'Are you following me, Captain?' demanded Michael, angry that his escapism had been so quickly interrupted.

'Following? No! I am Venetian, Mr Masson. Napoleon called this square the drawing-room of Europe. What more natural than for a Venetian on a brief visit home to stroll into his drawing-room to seek old acquaintance?'

'And we are the best you could manage?'

'You underrate your charms. Besides, if I sit here long enough, I shall see everyone I know in Venice. Another drink? You permit?'

· He snapped his fingers and ordered a repeat of the whole round.

'Nice to see that some of Mike's friends buy as well as drink,' observed Wilf.

'Oh Christ. The charm of the man,' said Wendy.

'How's the case going, Captain?' asked Bob.

'Please, no shop,' interposed Molly.

'Forgive me, I shall try not to bore you,' said Contarini. 'There has been progress. The young man, Aristide Roussel . . .'

'You've found him?' interrupted Sarah.

'Yes. We have found him. Tell me, Mr Masson, you did not by chance know where he was staying?'

'No idea,' said Michael. 'How should I?'

'Of course. And anyone else here? Did anyone know?'

There was no reply. Contarini nodded.

'I see. Mr Masson, when you were so regrettably assaulted this morning, was anything taken from you?'

'I don't know. I didn't really look. I've got my passport and . . .'

'Is this yours?'

The captain held out a brown leather billfold. Michael took it gingerly and examined it with care, remembering the last occasion Contarini had produced one of his possessions.

'Yes. I think it is. I'm sure of it.'

'You didn't miss it.'

'No. I just thought I'd left it in the bedroom. I'm pretty careless . . .'

'Yes. I recall. Like the lighter.'

'Yes. Well, not really. I always carry money loose in my pockets, I'm afraid. This, well, there might have been a thousand lire in it. Nothing more.'

'So, you thought you had lost it. Like the lighter,' said Contarini. 'You are indeed a careless man. Tell me; this man, Aristide, was he ever in your bedroom at the Leonardo.'

Michael and Sarah exchanged glances.

'Yes,' said Sarah firmly. 'He was. They – he and Mr Dunkerley – asked if they could leave their luggage there for safe keeping. Aristide went to collect it later.'

'By himself?'

'I told her she was crazy,' observed Wendy. 'I know a crook when I see one. I should do. I've had the practice.'

'What's all this mean?' asked Bob. 'Do you think this lad, Aristide, had something to do with the killing?'

'It seems possible, yes.'

'Well,' said Bob with the gloomy envy of one who knows for certain that the interview rooms of continental police stations are fitted with built-in thumbscrews, 'no doubt you'll soon persuade him to talk.'

'Difficult,' said Contarini. 'Regrettably he is dead.'

The music halted once more and all around them people applauded. It was as if they were clapping the captain's announcement.

'Dead?' said Sarah. 'Oh no.'

'Silly sod. I should have let him drown,' said Wendy.

'If the poor bastard's dead, he must be guilty of *everything*,' laughed Wilf. 'That's police thinking. Waste not, want not.'

Molly said nothing.

'Let's have another drink,' said Michael.

'What of?' said Bob.

'Whatever you want,' answered Michael.

'No. I meant, what'd he die of?'

'He bled to death,' said Contarini. 'There had been a struggle. He was hit with a broken chair, or perhaps fell on it. It pierced his spleen.'

'Ugh,' said Wendy, stubbing out a cigarette and immediately lighting another.

'Any leads?' asked Bob.

'Nothing definite. The struggle was heard but no one investigated. It is not the kind of area where you poke your eyes into other people's business. A little girl wandered in later and found him. He was dead then. The girl said she had seen a lady enter earlier, then a man.'

'Ah,' said Bob. 'Descriptions?'

Contarini shrugged.

'The lady we are not sure of. Even her existence is in doubt. The child has visions, or at least her parents are training her up to have a vision, perhaps perform a miracle. It is not uncommon, creates a small stir, provides an income while the interest lasts.'

'Monstrous!' said Sarah.

'I think so. Anyway the girl says it may have been the Virgin Mary. She is pretty certain there was a halo. It is hardly evidence!'

'And the man?'

'That's more promising. More reality, less vision. A fat man with a stubby beard and blue-tinted glasses does not transform so easily to a saint.'

'Dunkerley!' said Bob and Wilf together.

'It may be so,' said Contarini. 'My men are looking for him now.'

'But what about this Rimini business?' insisted Bob.

'Possibly a connection. This Roussel was a violent man, this we know. The evidence suggests he attacked Mr Masson today. A knife was found in his belongings. We are examining it and his clothes too. When Guido Falcone was stabbed, there was much bleeding. Some traces may remain even after a washing. Signora Masson.'

'Yes?' said Sarah.

'I would be grateful if you would identify the shirt you gave to Roussel. There is only one with an English label, but your confirmation is needed.'

'Of course,' said Sarah.

Michael had attracted the waiter and ordered another round despite an inward shudder at the thought of the cost. The music had resumed, a lush romantic piece he almost recognized. As the waiter set the drinks on the table, the rich surge of melody was interrupted, a trumpet hiccoughed and missed a bar, other instruments wandered slightly from the melodic line and voices could be heard above the orchestra.

'What's happening?' asked Molly.

'I don't know,' said Wilf. 'But one thing's sure in this

place – they'll find a way of charging us for it!'

Whatever it was, the band now seemed free of it and euphony was restored on the dais, but in the crowd a ripple of chatter and laughter marked the progress of the disruptive element across the piazza.

'I dreamt that I dwelt in marble halls,' sang a rather pleasant lyric tenor, and the crowd parted to reveal Dunkerley, his face alight with the wonder of his own singing, being helped along by a policeman who was still at the stage of finding this drunk amusing.

'Hey, *poliziotto*!' cried Contarini rudely. The man looked angrily in their direction, Contarini spoke a few sharp words which were enough to convince the policeman of his authority, and Dunkerley was pushed towards their table.

Contarini stared at him narrowly as though convincing himself of his identity. Dunkerley returned the stare boldly and winked. Then his gaze flickered round the rest of the group.

'All together, eh? Enjoying yourselves, eh? Doesn't last long, does it? A few days' boozing and screwing and getting your titties tanned; bang! there goes your holiday. Back to England, home and respectability, with all your best holiday slides locked away up here, inside your mind, bring 'em out at dead of night when your better half's asleep, or on the bus to work in the morning! Something for the winter, keeps you going. Well, I'll tell you something; I'll tell you; you can keep it! *All* of it! Winters and woollies and no coal and income tax and reds under every fucking bed. Me, I know when I'm well off. We'll be in the sun, me and Aristide, Tunisia, perhaps, Morocco, follow the sun, eighty in the shade, that's the life for Ari and me . . .'

'Mr Dunkerley,' said Contarini.

Sarah grasped Michael's hand and held it tight. For once he shared her sympathy. Poor sod.

'Why, hello there! Fabian of the Yard. Is my gondola double parked?'

'Your friend, Monsieur Roussel, Aristide.'

Everyone was looking away except Bob and Contarini.

Only policemen watch your face when they tell you about death.

'What about him? Come to his senses yet? He had it coming, but never worry about us. He'll come to his senses.'

He should flee, thought Michael. The news will destroy him. He should flee to the top of the campanile, there peer out over the festive lights of the square till they dance in the dark like fireflies. Then big close-up, Dunkerley's face through the grille, the music from the band rises to him, throbbing, gay. He clambers, like some great sad captive ape, up the protective grille till he reaches the gap. It is not easy to manoeuvre that bulk through, but he does it. He hangs outside for a moment, then lets himself go. Soundlessly, in slow motion the body falls, turning twice in the air. As it hits the ground the camera rushes back up the campanile, borne on a fountain of shrieks then freezes on the final shot, the golden angel which stands on top of the tower, against a sky of unflawed blue . . .

'He is dead,' said Contarini. 'Aristide Roussel is dead.'

'Oh Christ!' said Dunkerley and, doubling up, he vomited all over the table.

Half way down the green light corridor a Customs official halted their progress.

'Sir. Madam. You are together? Would you mind stepping over here? You have read and understood the regulations, I take it?'

'Oh damn! Why us?' demanded Michael, looking after the fast disappearing back of Wilf whose bag was almost certainly weighed down with gallons of illicit booze.

'Could you tell me if you have brought any of the items on the list into the country?'

'No, we bloody well haven't. I mean, only what we're allowed. That's why we're coming out through this exit. I thought that was the whole idea.'

'Michael, please.'

Sarah smiled beguilingly at the Customs man. Michael had noticed that any sign of antagonism from himself towards authority figures invariably brought out this gentle condescension in his wife, whereas whenever he tried the friendly approach, she would quickly begin to complain about neo-fascist attitudes.

The Customs officer smiled back.

'Would you open your cases, please?'

They did so and watched in silence as the man began to remove articles one by one, squeezing, probing, unfolding. A carton of cigarettes caught his interest. When he put it down, Michael reached across, tore it open, removed a packet and opened it.

'Smoke?' he said.

The Customs officer continued searching without reply. Sarah's neat efficient packing was now completely spoilt but she did not seem to mind. Looking at the growing mound of clothes on the table top, Michael was reminded of the pitifully scant pile of Aristide's possessions laid out in the police headquarters in Venice. He had let Sarah identify and sign for the clothing the dead man had borrowed while he concentrated on trying to pump Contarini for information.

The captain had been surprisingly co-operative, conciliatory almost, as though, having decided Michael was clear of suspicion, he had begun to worry about possible complaints about his behaviour. Michael found it amusing, especially as he suspected an Italian in England could expect a much rougher passage if he ever fell into Bob's hands.

'The Frenchman, yes, he probably killed Falcone. Motive? Who knows? Roussel was a sexual deviant so perhaps having had his advances repulsed, he became angry. Such cases are not uncommon. But he had a knife which would fit the wounds on the boy, some traces of blood were found, we had enough, not to charge him perhaps, but to press him strongly for a confession.'

'In the Roman Catholic sense?' said Michael drily.

'*Scusi?* Ah yes, I remember. In every sense, Signore Masson. But he is dead and the law has no more interest in him. Except as he was connected with the other, Dunkerley.'

'What will happen to him?'

'Who knows? Who cares? He and his kind, *vitelloni* eh? He claims it was accidental. I think he may be telling the truth. What will happen now? A man from your consulate came to see him.'

'They do occasionally take notice, then?' said Michael.

'I think so. Dunkerley says he was at school with this man. If so, is it not strange? The man looked so unhappy I feel it may be true! So perhaps English diplomacy will extract Dunkerley from our grasp, for – what is it you say? – for old times' sake.'

'I hope so,' said Michael.

'You hope? That is generous. They are not nice people, this old man, the dead one. Why did he attack you, I

wonder? There are still mysteries. Here is Signora
Masson. You have the clothes? Good. Be careful who you
loan them to in future. Perhaps I may see you when next
I come to England.'

'Delighted,' said Michael. 'I'll take you to the cinema.
Fred Astaire.'

'Astaire? That would be superb! Are there still cinemas
where his films are shown? Remember *Carefree*? What is it
you say? They don't make films like that any more!'

The rest of the holiday had been subdued, but pleasant
enough. He and Sarah had spent most of their time
together viewing without concern the increasing frag-
mentation of the rest of the group. Now they were home
and already it was all beginning to fade like last week's
second feature. Venice alone remained, powerful, un-
erasable, unique.

The officer had finished at last and was ostentatiously
helping Sarah to re-pack. Michael ground out his
cigarette and began shovelling his clothes back into the
case, making no effort to emulate the neat way in which
Sarah had packed them for the homeward journey.
Almost finished, he paused and looked into his case with
some puzzlement.

'Thank you very much,' said Sarah. 'Ready, darling?'

'I think so. This shirt. Is it mine?'

'Let me see,' said Sarah. 'Yes, of course.'

'It doesn't look like mine. I mean the colour's similar,
but . . . it doesn't even look like a Marks and Sparks
style though it's got the label.'

'Of course it's yours. Do come on.'

Sarah raised her eyebrows in mock exasperation at the
Customs man, who smiled.

'I must have forgotten,' said Michael as they walked
out into the main concourse of the airport.

'It's a useful talent,' observed Sarah. She rummaged in
her handbag, noting that the bell-necklace had got
tangled up with her little quick-repair set.

'Here's the car park ticket,' she said. 'I'll wait here,
shall I?'

'He's gone,' said a flat all-too-familiar voice.

'Oh Christ,' said Michael, looking unwelcomingly at Wendy who had approached them unawares.

'Who's gone?'

'Wilf. He just said to me, *Well, you've been wanting rid of me for a long time. Cheerioh, sweetie*, and went off. I saw him getting into a taxi. *She* was with him.'

'Who?'

'*Her*,' said Wendy as though she could not utter the name. But she pointed towards the main exit where Bob stood peering with complete bewilderment into the night.

'You mean Molly?' cried Michael in disbelief. 'You must be wrong.'

'Hush,' said Sarah. 'I'm sorry, Wendy. These things happen. And you did want to make a break.'

'It's you,' said Wendy, tears now trailing spoors of mascara down her whitened face. 'You told me to divorce him. You've driven him off. It's your fault.'

'Nonsense,' said Sarah briskly. 'You've got what you wanted. Now enjoy life. Come on, Michael. I'll walk to the car with you.'

She took Michael's arm in a firm grip and propelled him briskly across the room like an arrested criminal.

'But what shall I do?' cried Wendy. 'What shall I do?'

Michael's concern was diverted by the necessity of passing close to Bob. He felt pretty certain that almost anything he could say to the stricken policeman would invite a punch on the nose. Fortunately Bob solved the problem by offering no sign of recognition.

'You knew,' accused Michael, sucking in a chill draught of English night air.

'Everyone knew. You have no sensitivity about women. She's better off.'

'Which?'

'Both.'

'But what *will* Wendy do? Tonight I mean. She looks completely lost.'

'She'll manage. She'll have to at first, that's important. If she starts depending on someone now, she'll never make a life for herself. I'll ring her in a week. I've got her address.'

'Well,' said Michael, 'I suppose she can always ask a policeman.'

They walked on, shifting their cases from one hand to another as the weight grew unbearable. An aeroplane roared dismally into the low cloud and the damp wind pasted English litter against the mesh of the car park fence. The car when they spotted it looked familiar and welcoming, the first really *homely* thing Sarah had seen since landing.

Michael must have felt the same too for he sighed with pleasure as he slid into the driving seat and said, 'Well, that's that, then.'

'What?'

'*Abroad*. That's *abroad* safe behind us. Some close calls, but we made it. It's like an old-fashioned scenario, really. Hero and heroine emerge unscathed. No one gets hurt, no one who matters anyway. A harmless bit of escapism, quickly forgotten. Just another death in Venice.'

He switched on the engine, smiling as it fired first time despite its long stand in the open.

'No,' said Sarah.

'No what?'

'There's got to be an end. I mean, a real end, not just words on a screen and music swelling up and us going home to continue as before.'

Michael switched off the engine.

'What's up, love?' he asked. 'Bad news from Bangladesh?'

She slapped his face.

'Jesus Christ!' he said.

'Listen, Michael, and listen good,' she said. 'This isn't the best place in the world for a showdown, but it's better than at home where the children might hear. It's got to stop! All right, I'm not stupid, I know it's more than just a question of pulling yourself together. You'll need help. Well, I'll help, naturally, and if it comes to treatment, I know people, *useful* people; there's some advantage to being socially involved, you'll see.'

'What are you going on about?' he interrupted.

'About *you*, Michael, and what you are and what you do . . .'

'And what *is* that? Come on, love! The suspense is killing me. What am I supposed to have done?'

'Don't you *know*? Don't you really *know*?' she said in a voice so vibrantly earnest that he longed for a custard pie to thrust in her face.

'No! I don't bloody know! All I know is I'm tired of being married to Florence Freud, the People's Friend. I took you for better or worse, richer or poorer, in sickness or in health, but it didn't say anything about the rest of the sodding world!'

He had grown angry in spite of himself and his anger acted like the longed-for pie.

'You can say that?' she cried, her voice thickening with indignation. 'You can say that, after what I've done for you?'

'What?' he asked, with an effort reaching something like a George Sanders suavity of tone. '*What* have you done for me?'

'Oh, come on! That shirt . . . *this doesn't look like my shirt*, he says. How fortunate! Perhaps Federico Fellini changed them! Well, it was *me*. I nearly just took yours with me but I thought, no. That'll look really suspicious. I could see a stain on it, you see. I didn't know what it was, but I was worried. You worry me a lot, Michael. So I changed the labels with one of his. And I left your billfold, so they'd think he stole it. Perhaps in Rimini where he could have got your lighter. Or perhaps they'd think he beat you up in Venice.'

She was speaking defiantly and with growing speed as she realized that soon she would start crying. It had all been a very great strain, more than she'd appreciated.

'You mean you were *there*?' said Michael. 'At Aristide's?'

'Of course I was there! What does it matter? He was dead; well, dying. It didn't matter. He was a crook; they both were; Sydney told me; he tried to blackmail me about you . . .'

'But what were you doing there?' he asked. '*What?*'

'I was saving you!' she screamed, and felt the tears start.

'What from?'

'From the law! From Contarini! From yourself!'

'Ah!' he said. 'Ah. Great dialogue! So, so. I see. Bob the Bobby was right! I didn't screw that whore in Florence; no, I came back to Rimini and tried to pick up a boy on the beach, got into a fight with him and killed him. Yes, it's all coming back to me. The rich warm air, the strange sea-smells, the passionate rake of his nails across my shoulder. Ah! God, yes! It's all clear. I'm a repressed homosexual! That's how I got beaten up in Venice. I was trying to pick up a boy in a red shirt and he got angry and attacked me. But I quite enjoyed that too. Yes, yes, I see it. I'm a repressed masochist too. This is great, this is fine. It's all coming back now! And there's more! there's more! It was my vote that lost Labour the election in 1970! And I'm the man behind the Indian drought! Oh, hurry, hurry, patch me up with your needle and thread!'

He stopped and felt angry and ashamed and confused. Beside him in the dark car Sarah was weeping, not noisily as Wendy had wept on the far side of the bedroom wall, but in an effortless profusion.

'Please,' he said finally. 'Don't cry.'

'I can't stop,' she said.

'Yes, you can,' he said. 'Come on. Please try. I'm sorry for what I said . . .'

'Oh no,' she interposed quickly. 'Don't be. It was good to hear you being angry.'

'Was it?'

'Yes, really.'

'I'll do it more often. I suppose I should thank you really.'

'What for.'

'What you did, even though . . .'

'Yes?'

'Do you still think I did it? Any of it?'

She looked at him with that dreadful honesty which had always concealed her lack of charm.

'I don't know,' she said. 'Do you? It doesn't matter, really. What matters is tomorrow. There's a real life to

ive. You've been evading it, slipping away from it too
ong. You've got responsibilities, to me, to the kids, to the
community at large.'

'And mankind,' he prompted. 'Don't forget mankind.'

'Yes, that too,' she said, ignoring the bait. 'But start
small. Me and the children will do for starters. You're
valuable to us.'

He switched on the windscreen wipers to clear the gaze
but their breathing had steamed up the inside and he had
to rub with the back of his hand to get a view.

'But if I'm a criminal . . .' he mused.

'There's no such thing,' she said fiercely. 'It's a stale
concept. Crime is sickness. It should be treated, not
punished.'

'Yes,' he said. 'Of course. In that case . . .'

He laughed suddenly and took her hand.

'You've stopped crying,' he said.

'Please, Michael. Will you try?'

'You're going to stay with me? Not leave me?'

'Never!' she said. 'I've too much at stake.'

'Certain?'

'Oh *yes*.'

'All right then. I'll try anything once.'

'Starting as soon as we get home? Starting tomorrow?'

'Tomorrow?'

'Yes. Tomorrow,' she insisted.

Silently he nodded.

Sarah regarded him doubtingly and longingly. Was he
really worth it? she wondered. What *was* he, really? What
was *she*, for that matter. No better, certainly, or could she
remember without shame the things she had done? One
part of her mind had been very much aware of that ever-
growing pool of blood beneath that slack but still living
body, but the other part, the major part, the part that
normally dealt with questions of morality and responsibility, that had somehow been totally occupied by the
careful snip of her tiny scissors and the precise repetition
of her neat stitches.

Perhaps it was callousness not sensitivity which enabled
her to come so close to the woes of the world.

Well, it was good to discover new truths about oneself. Recognition must preface regeneration. She hoped whatever it was Michael must recognize would be bearable to him. Psychiatry was about *Doppelgänger*. And there were worse shocks than a confrontation with yourself. An English police court, for instance, or a beating up which left you crippled. Thank God the crisis had come in Venice! For the crisis had come, she was convinced of that. The knowledge that she would never leave him must be his greatest support. He might still be in trouble, but he was ready to be helped. She could see it in his face, in the way he was gazing ahead hopefully, longingly.

He too was eager for tomorrow.

Michael gazed ahead, hopefully, longingly.

The screen was silvering once more and shapes and shadows formed where his hand had passed.

Long shot. The ocean. Night. Out towards the misty horizon a vague, bulky figure stirs uneasily. The wind blows in squally gusts. Waves race towards the shore.

Medium shot. The shore. Dawn. A paddle-boat bob in the shallows. Two figures occupy the seats. They turn their heads and look towards the camera. The red-shirted youth says something to the bearded man in the blue-tinted glasses. They both laugh, but not mockingly, then begin to paddle out to sea.

Big close-up. Michael's face against a wind-torn sky.

Michael: TOMORROW IS ANOTHER DAY.